WINTER TERRITORY

A JACK WIDOW THRILLER

SCOTT BLADE

Black Lion Media

1

THE MAN WAS ABOUT twenty-five years old and freezing.

The cold pierced through his skin and shot straight to his bones. The temperatures outside dipped into the low twenties, and the winter hadn't even come on yet. Not fully. It was still the middle of November, but the mountaintops were snowcapped, and the sky was wet with the cold, dewy feeling that came with high altitudes and frigid skies. Which exactly described his location—high up in a stark, cold winter. He was in the Absaroka Mountain Range, a part of the Rockies. The elevation was somewhere around thirteen thousand feet, but he wasn't sure of the exact number.

The man was hiding out in a familiar place—a place he used to hide when he was young. He felt safe there.

Outside, the night wind blew and battered the ruggedly built wooden structure. It was primitive, but had endured the cold winters for many, many years. For the moment, nothing and no one would find him. The man was safe, but it wouldn't be for long. He had nowhere else to go. He had run out of options and time.

They were coming for him, and they would come in hot with guns blazing. They would kill him for sure—no doubt about it. He had been running for days, and he knew he would come face-to-face with them soon enough. His cover had been blown all to hell and back.

No changing that now. No changing the past.

But that wasn't the thing that worried him at the moment. The thing that was the immediate danger wasn't the guys coming to kill him for betraying them. It wasn't the fact that they had trusted him, and he had turned on them. It wasn't the dangerous enemies who had once terrified him. The immediate danger wasn't the contents of the stolen bullet-proof briefcase that was covered in dirt and grime and still damp from being dragged through the snowy terrain.

The immediate danger that ate away at him was that he was starving. He hadn't eaten in days, so many days that he had no idea when the last time was.

Two weeks ago, he had been on a military stealth helicopter on his way into Mexico, or maybe back from Mexico, across the Mexican–United States border. He couldn't remember for sure. The details were fuzzy because his thinking was muddled. Five or six or seven days without food will do that to a man. He tried to remember his training, his tradecraft, but all he could focus on was the stealth helicopter.

He had thought it was such a cool thing. It was a Comanche RAH-70, the most terrifying machine he had ever seen. Reports from around the world had claimed that highly modified Black Hawk UH-60s were the stealth helicopters used in the raid on Osama bin Laden's compound in 2011. He hadn't been there in 2011—he had been far too young at the time to have been involved in that operation—but he had top secret clearance and was privy to knowledge that the helicopters used were, in fact, Comanche's RAH-70s, cousins of the RAH-66.

Public knowledge said that the Comanche helicopters had been canceled way back in 2004. The programs were too expensive for the US military, but not for his employer. His employer had found a use for them and had financed dozens of them to be created for stealth missions. They were housed in strategic military installations all around the world. Military service personnel were restricted from accessing them. Authorized persons had been told never to reveal any details about them to anyone.

The helicopter was a remarkable machine with deadly and accurate machine guns attached. It was equipped with special side turret-style machine guns based on the Vulcan-style gun and could fire M50 ammunition at fifteen hundred rounds per minute. The ammunition housed five hundred rounds and could be reloaded in fifteen minutes.

The man knew this information not because of his military training, but because of his tradecraft. Although now he questioned the statistics and details in his mind because he knew one thing for certain—he was starving, and the lack of sustenance in his body was causing him to lose focus and reasoning. He tried desperately to concentrate on the details of the stealth helicopter. And it helped. But he was still starving.

He was in one of the richest states in the country, and at that moment, he was a rich man. He was richer than he had been five or six or seven days ago because of the value of the contents of the security briefcase in his possession.

Next to the man was a Beretta nine millimeter, a service weapon given to him just before his secret mission. It rested on top of a closed shoebox next to him in close grabbing distance. The safety was on, but that could change quickly. The shoebox was stacked on top of a large appliance box that held old items from a childhood long past.

The room the man was in was dark and dank and not well insulated. Spiders indigenous to the region crawled in the far corner of the ceiling. They crawled in the shadows of a swinging bulb that hung down on a long cord and swayed back and forth in a curved arc from west to north. A wind that chilled the room blew the bulb from side to side. The man could hear a faint whistle that sounded with the gusts of wind from the outside terrain.

The man was sitting on the floor with his back to the wall. He craned his neck to look out of a snow-covered, shuttered window above his head. He had to press his body up against the wall and use his arms to hoist himself up just to see. Billions of stars shimmered across the stretch of sky. The ground was covered in snow, but the night sky was clear and dark blue and picturesque, like the wallpaper on a desktop computer. Perhaps on a computer back in Langley, Virginia, which was where he had lived for the last year of his life.

The man leaned forward some more and looked straight down at the front of the house. He couldn't see the front door from his position, but he was over two stories up, and he could see more than a hundred yards down the steep land in front of him. Behind him were dense trees and then the edge of a rugged mountain. He wasn't much worried about men coming for him from that direction. He figured these guys would just come straight up the long, wide driveway if they could find it. The snow had covered it over, leaving no signs of where it used to be. More than likely, his enemies would come in by snowmobile, and he would hear their engines in the dead silence around him. The noise would echo and bounce off the far-off trees or the sides of the mountains. No way could anyone surprise him on a snowmobile. The only alternative means of transportation would've been horses. The snow on the ground wasn't deep enough to prevent them from riding on horseback up the track.

Either way, it wouldn't matter. He was ready. His main problem wasn't how they would come for him, but when.

The owner of the house didn't know he was there. He was hiding out. He prayed he wouldn't be discovered. The last thing he wanted to do was involve innocent people.

Just then, he heard a noise, a creaking on the staircase below him. He stretched back up and craned his head to look out the window. He couldn't see the front door because of the huge porch, a fact he had forgotten. Then he remembered he had just looked down only moments ago.

The man heard more noises from below him. He heard footsteps growing louder and louder. A moment later, someone was on the floor beneath him, and then he heard a chair moving across the floor and light footsteps as if someone had climbed the chair and reached up for the rope to the attic door. He heard the creaks of his frozen bones as he twisted to look at the trapdoor and then the squeaking of springs from the door itself as someone pulled it down. The sound was deafening in the house's silence.

He grabbed his Beretta and quickly pointed it in the direction of the attic door as it was pulled downward. Light flashed in through the crack and up onto the ceiling above him. Soon it filled half of the attic. He wanted to slide over to hide behind some of the larger boxes, but he couldn't really move his legs. He had lost feeling in them some time ago but couldn't remember when. He had forgotten they were paralyzed, but not permanently. It was from exhaustion.

The trapdoor went down all the way, and the folding staircase attached plopped down below. The man heard the creak of the wooden ladder as someone climbed it. A head stuck up into the attic, and a body followed. The tiny figure in front of him scanned across the attic and the boxes until their eyes connected.

The man lowered his Beretta when he saw a small boy, approximately six years of age. The boy glowered at him peculiarly. Most likely a combination of fright because of the gun and then recognition.

The man had been in and out of sleep for days and had spent so much energy in guarding himself, holding the Beretta up, that before he knew it, his eyes closed under the heavy weight of his eyelids.

2

JACK WIDOW WAS DOING what he loved best—wandering without a care in the world. This was what he thought was true freedom. A lifetime of doing as he was told had turned him into a man who no longer listened to anyone. He did as he wanted and went where he pleased.

Widow had spent the last several months doing more and seeing more of his home country than he had ever done or seen in his entire life. He had traveled from Mississippi, a place that seemed so far away and long ago in his memory, through seven states, across hundreds of highways, around thousands of cloverleaves, and over the southern part of the Rocky Mountains. He'd traveled all the way west until he couldn't go any farther unless he started swimming or chartered a boat or stole a submarine or bought a plane ticket. And even then, he was out of states except for Hawaii and Alaska, depending on whether you considered them to be west.

Over the last year, he had discovered three addictions. The first was the open road. There was nothing like the freedom of the American frontier. The second was coffee. Coffee was a drug he couldn't explain. Perhaps it was from being a Navy cop. Perhaps not. Or maybe it was just a drug that did what drugs do and did it well—it created an addiction. Whatever the case was, he didn't care. And the third was that he was constantly picking up old paperback books and reading them along his travels.

He had slept only about five hours the night before because he had met a girl named Farrah in Salt Lake City. The only person he had known with that name was the actress Farrah Fawcett, but when he'd asked the girl about it, she had denied being named after her. She told him she had been asked that question for her entire life but claimed never to have even seen a Farrah Fawcett film. As the girl was only twenty-four years old, that was probably true. Farrah had been dead for years and hadn't really done any acting in decades. The only thing Widow knew her from was *Charlie's Angels*, a horrible show in his opinion, from before he was born.

Farrah—the twenty-four-year-old and not the actress—had been a lot of fun for Widow. She was a part-time waitress and student, not at the University of Utah but at a community college. She was taking night classes to be a nurse, a trade that Widow admired. He admired anyone who was in the profession of helping others. The military, criminal justice, firefighting, the medical field, and even the clergy were all trades he respected.

Farrah was the complete opposite of Farrah Fawcett, but that didn't mean she wasn't gorgeous. She was absolutely gorgeous, far more so than the 1970s actress. At least that was Widow's conclusion. Farrah was six feet tall. She was dark-skinned with long, straight black hair and even longer legs. She was toned, but not in the way of someone who was into fitness. It was more of a youthful way, the way you are when you have good genes.

Widow had met Farrah while she was working at a local bar. She had thought it was odd that he was reading a book in a bar, and they struck up a conversation. He had asked her to have a drink after her shift ended, which they did. His time on the road had been lonely. Not that the isolation didn't appeal to him as well. He liked to be alone. And there was something romantic and resolute about wandering. He found peace. Widow accepted the aloneness, but finding the occasional friend was something he looked forward to.

After they had a beer together—some local craft brew— Farrah had invited Widow back to her place for another beer, which turned the one beer into an all-night thing, which was okay by him.

In the morning, Widow put his clothes on and said goodbye to Farrah as she slept. He wasn't sure if she had heard him or not, and it hadn't mattered. He was ready to be on his way.

He left her asleep in her bed in her ground-level apartment and locked the door behind him. He left without a phone number or without leaving her one in return. No email. No forwarding address. There was no point. He had no phone. No email. No address.

Widow had been born in Mississippi to a single mom. She was an ex-Marine, which meant she was still a Marine. She was also the sheriff of the town in which Widow had grown up in until six months ago when she had been murdered while investigating a series of disappearances of beautiful women.

Widow had left his assignment as an undercover Navy cop to investigate her death, returning to the small town he'd grown up in. No one remembered him because he had left home when he was eighteen and joined the Navy. He'd spent sixteen years away from home and never called or wrote or spoke to his mother. His last two memories of her were the day she died and sixteen years before, when they had fought one of those life-changing fights. She'd admitted to lying to him his entire life about his father.

Widow had grown up thinking that his father had been a military war hero, a soldier who had died defending his country. But when he turned eighteen, she told him the truth. His father had been a drifter, just some guy. Widow had wanted to escape small-town life for his entire child-hood, and that fight with his mother led him to run away with the Navy. Originally, he had planned to call her, but one month turned into two and then into six. Six months turned into a year, which turned into many years.

American families.

By the time sixteen years had passed, it took a tragedy for him to return home. When he returned to his old town, the people there had thought of him as a drifter. So he continued on to the town in which his mother had died and kept his drifter persona intact.

Widow knew about undercover work—that's what he did for NCIS. He stayed undercover to find out who shot his mother, and that led him down a dark path. At the end of which, he came face-to-face with a conspiracy he'd much rather forget.

After his mother died, the NCIS told him he had to come back. That was his only choice, but Widow decided it was time to make his own choices. He put one foot in front of the other and never looked back.

What started as a quest to find the person responsible for shooting his sheriff mother had turned into a full-blown obsession, which turned into a way of life.

Along the way, Widow realized that the first part of his life had been to follow in his mother's footsteps. She was a Marine and a cop, and he had become a Navy SEAL and a cop. Now in the second half of his life, he was a drifter, like the father he had never known. Now he was literally following in his father's footsteps.

No possessions had been Widow's thing. It was because, in the Navy, Widow had carried gear everywhere he went. He had been trained to carry tremendous weight. After he joined the NCIS and went undercover with a secret unit, he had carried more than physical things with him. Living a double life had taken a toll on him. Now he carried nothing.

Widow didn't want possessions. Possessions meant commitment and things to carry and store. In Widow's mind, things to carry meant baggage, and baggage could hold you down and hold you back.

The things Widow carried now were his passport, his debit card, and a wad of cash, which was four hundred fifty-eight dollars at that moment. He tried to carry cash-money on him. He never knew when he would need quick access to it. In addition, using cash provided a lot more anonymity than using his debit card. And he liked anonymity.

The only other item he carried was a foldable toothbrush, which looked like a blue barber-style shaving blade. Instead of a blade that snicked out of the handle, there was a tooth-brush. The bristles and plastic head folded down into the handle and flipped out like a switchblade. He carried the toothbrush but replaced it fairly often. Toothbrushes could be bought at any drugstore.

On the morning after Widow left Farrah for Salt Lake City, he ventured out to visit the unique attractions around the city, including the Temple Square gardens, thirty-five acres of land downtown that headquartered the Mormon Church. The gardens were world famous and had two hundred and fifty flower beds and seven hundred different plants from all across the planet. The gardens were replanted and redesigned every year, and it took hundreds of volunteers to finish them. But Widow couldn't get in to see them because the garden was only open in the summer, and tours were by appointment only.

So he spent the afternoon on a ritual he completed either daily or weekly, depending on where he was and how dirty he had gotten. He went to a cheap-looking old barbershop and said hello to an old guy with a jarhead haircut and photographs of himself with other guys, doing guy things, that were pinned all over a bulletin board near the entrance. The old guy said hello back and asked if Widow needed a cut. Widow nodded and told him he would like a buzz cut.

On the road, Widow had discovered the benefits of keeping his hair short, and he had quickly shed the long-haired look. Of course, in the winter months, it would make sense to let it grow long, but Widow was still getting used to the drifter lifestyle. For the last six months, he had been getting his head buzzed short and hadn't yet thought about the winter. He had figured he'd spend it in California, but he had gotten there earlier than he'd thought he would. Part of this new nomadic life was going with the flow, and the flow had turned him around at the Pacific Ocean.

After the jarhead barber had cut his hair short, Widow got out of the chair, paid the man, and thanked him. Then he left the barbershop and walked down the street along a cracked cement sidewalk to a side of town that was less than pristine. Potholes riddled the street, and old cars were parked along the street. Leaning telephone poles besieged the area like reminders of a forgotten time.

Widow walked on until he found what he was looking for, an old consignment store called America's Clothing Store. Not a catchy name for a consignment store, but Widow wasn't looking for trendy. He was looking for cheap.

Another thing he'd discovered was buying cheap clothes was better than owning one pair and rewashing them all the time. Laundromats aren't cheap. Detergent isn't cheap. Buying new clothes, wearing them, and tossing them in a Salvation Army bin after was like being a part of a subscription service. In his mind, it was like Netflix for clothes. He'd buy new ones, wear them, recycle them, and someone else would use them.

He walked into the store and nodded at a cute girl behind the counter. She was folding clothes and nodded and smiled back at him. He guessed she was barely an adult. She looked like a mixture of Asian and white. The girl wore a multicolored striped top with mostly gray in it and black chinos. She was petite, probably five foot one. Her hair was shorter than shoulder length, dyed pink, and shaved on one side. To Widow, she looked like a modern punk rocker, a style that seemed to return.

Traveling from state to state, city to city, Widow had come across young people of all types. In the urban areas, he'd noticed similar hairstyles, especially among girls. Although he was from a southern state, a conservative state, Widow couldn't complain about the new look. In fact, on her, it looked damn good.

He began wandering around the store. They didn't have a big and tall section—he had found that most places didn't. The big and tall sections of America hadn't vanished—there were plenty of them out there—but most of the stores that catered to bigger people had become specialty stores. Expensive specialty stores. So Widow had often settled for XXL or XXXL if he could find it in tops. Fitting his waist hadn't been a problem because he had a thin waist for a guy his size—thirty-four inches, but he was six four with long legs and needed pants that were long enough. Usually, he'd buy a size thirty-six and let them ride on his hips.

Widow headed to the pants section and searched around. He looked at jeans first and found a pair of Levi carpenter jeans, size thirty-five. The legs were long. He grabbed them and walked over to look at the tops. He sifted through the selections and pulled out a long-sleeved white shirt. Then he turned and started toward a wall of shoes on display, but before he got there, he saw a nice gray fleece vest from the corner of his eye. He stopped and looked it over. He was thinking about heading northeast and realized he had no winter gear, and it was now the beginning of November.

He grabbed the fleece and looked at the tag. It was only an XXL, but it was a sleeveless vest, so he didn't need to worry about it having long sleeves that reached only to his fore-arms. Widow had abnormally long arms—long arms and long legs. His mother was tiny, so he assumed he had inher-ited them from his unknown father.

Widow grabbed his clothes and went over to the fitting room, which was in the back of the store. He dipped into a little hallway and came face-to-face with a young black girl who was barely out of high school. Like the girl from the front, she also had a punk rocker look about her. No pink hair, but she had three nose piercings and those huge pieces in her earlobes that looked like rims for a truck. They were black and rubbery looking. They opened her ear lobes up to a size big enough to slide his pinkie through, which was more like the size of a gun barrel.

She asked, "How are you, sir? Want to try those on?"

Widow said, "Yes."

"How many items do you have?"

"I have three, but I want to grab a pair of shoes and socks, too. Can I leave these with you?"

She said, "Here, I'll take them and set you up in a fitting room."

She reached out with tiny coffee-colored hands and took his three items. She had to use both arms to carry them, and even then, she was swallowed up like a newborn wrapped in king-sized sheets.

Widow turned and walked over to the shoes. He paced back and forth, looking at them, studying them. With shoes, he had only one goal on his mind, and that was to locate a size fourteen, which was his shoe size. Locating a comfortable shoe was one of the hardest things about being a little taller than average.

He had walked one way up the aisle and then back again when he realized that the bigger sizes were all the way at the top of the wall.

Widow looked at the small selection of shoes in size fourteen. His choices were pretty slim. There wasn't much there, not much at all. Not in the way of comfortable shoes. But he had found it was better to look at the work shoes and boots. There was usually a larger selection of them. He picked up a pair of plain black boots that were comparable to Timberlands but without the name brand. The boots were worn, but still in good shape. He took them and returned to the fitting room where the young clerk had hung his clothes. She handed him a white-and-yellow tag that said "4" in a big block font, showing how many items he had with him in the dressing room.

He went into the booth and closed the door, tried on the clothes. Everything fit pretty well, including the long-sleeved white shirt. Widow rolled the sleeves down over his forearms and looked in the mirror. He looked okay. He ripped the tags off all the items and pulled the size stickers off, and walked out wearing them

The girl looked him up, and down, smiled. She said, "Nice. Everything looks good."

"Thanks. I'll take them. I'm just going to wear them out."

The girl said, "That's fine. Where're your old clothes?"

"Right," he said. Then he turned and went back into the room and picked up his old clothes and shoes and the tag she had given him, and he came back out.

He handed her the tag, and she said, "If you take them to the front, Shelly will ring you up. Have a nice day."

Widow smiled and stayed quiet. He went to the register and paid for his new clothes, and walked out of the store. He stopped just outside the front door and turned to a Good-will bin that looked like a giant blue city garbage can with a slot to throw old clothes in.

Widow bunched up his old clothes and tossed them in—no reason to waste them.

Then he turned and looked at the shadows on the ground. The time matched what he guessed it to be, which was about 2:45 in the afternoon. One skill SEAL training had taught him was how to tell time by the sun's shadows. He had found that this skill wasn't completely necessary since he liked watches, especially tactical ones, but he wasn't wearing one at the moment.

He had lost his watch. Probably left it in a motel room somewhere, or maybe he left it at Farrah's. He thought about looking for a new one, but not from a consignment store.

He shrugged and figured he didn't need a watch. What was the point in knowing the time when you were always free?

3

THE NUMBER on the side of the building was 113 Main Street, and the building was a little country diner called Terry's Diner. Nothing special about it.

The address was 113, but the guy sitting in the booth by the window wondered why it was 113. The number made no sense because there wasn't a 112 or any other addresses on the street. Main Street in Tower Junction, Wyoming, was really like the only street. The other streets snaked off of it like little streams feeding off one slightly larger river.

The guy dressed far too nice to be a local. He wore cowboy boots, a cowboy hat, and a black suit. His clothes looked expensive because they were expensive. They had probably been bought in Texas or New Mexico. That was what Aubree thought.

Aubree was the youngest waitress who worked at the diner. She had just turned eighteen less than two weeks ago.

Today was her first shift on the floor by herself, but the whole waitress thing wasn't that hard. You greeted people, took their orders, and wrote them down on a ticket for the cook. He made the orders and stabbed the ticket on a spindle when it was ready. Then you brought it out to the guest. Not a big deal. And the menu was pretty plain. It was an all-American diet: cheeseburgers, soups, salads. No seafood. No pasta. But there was chicken on the menu and even a chicken sandwich. No fried foods except for French fries, and even they weren't really fried. They were microwaved, but Aubree was taught that there was no reason to tell the guest about how the fries were cooked.

She had greeted the guy sitting by the window, but all he had wanted was coffee and nothing else. The guy wore nice clothes, but that wasn't the thing that really stuck out to Aubree. The thing that really struck her was that he would've been good-looking for an older guy, except that he had a vicious deep-set scar that ran jagged across his face like someone had come at him with a chainsaw and skimmed the outside of his face. His left eye was completely grayed out like a blind man's, and the left part of his nose and left nostril were missing. The only thing that was left was a black hole shaped like a tiny triangle.

The guy's right eye was an amazing ice-blue color, like the middle of the ocean. He had silver-and-gray hair slicked back, creating the perfect style. He also had a beard that was peppered with black-and-gray hair.

The guy was probably in his late forties, not an old guy, not like a grandfather, but close to her dad's age.

Most of what Aubree could see about the guy was the good side of his face, and there was nothing wrong with that. But when she brought him his coffee, he turned his features directly to her, and she swallowed hard when she saw the hole on the one half of his nose. The rest of the scar had faded into his hairline perfectly at the top of his head, and it barely scraped across his upper lip. It left a slight cleft that wasn't bad, not at all. One time in high school, Aubree had to "volunteer" at a homeless shelter with other students who were a part of the local church. At this function, she had seen a guy with the upper part of his lip and teeth completely missing. The guy had tried to grow a mustache over it, but it was still visible.

Aubree remembered being told by her teacher to stop staring, but she couldn't help it. She watched the guy eat, which sickened her to her stomach. She felt bad about that later. After all, the guy wore a denim vest with military and veteran patches all over it. He had served in Vietnam or some war that happened long before she had been born.

The guy in the booth at the window accepted the coffee from her and never touched it.

He never looked back at her again. He just sat and stared out the window, like he was waiting for something or someone.

The guy had a serious way about him, like he was ex-military or a cop or both.

Other than the cowboy hat, which rested on the table in front of him, and the boots, the guy really didn't fit in. Besides Tower Junction being a small town and the fact that Aubree knew almost everyone in it, the guy stood out. And that wasn't because of the scar. It was more than that, but Aubree couldn't explain it.

Whatever the guy was waiting on, it was clear there was something on his mind. Something that was important, like he was waiting on a miracle—some outside force to answer his prayers.

4

THE SKY WAS LIGHT BLUE. Huge lenticular clouds hovered over the horizon. The weather wasn't bad, not yet, but Widow knew it was on the way. He had left Utah and hiked west and then north into Twin Falls. That was when he had been grateful for the fleece, because the weather had gotten colder—much colder. On the outskirts of Twin Falls, he had seen a digital bank sign that read the time and the temperature in a bright green color. The temperature had been forty-six degrees, which wasn't that cold, not like other places he'd been, but the night was approaching, and he was going higher in elevation. It was going to get colder. No question.

Widow had walked Highway 20 for thirty minutes, heading in a northeasterly direction, when he was finally picked up by an old guy, maybe in his sixties, with a thick beard and a completely bald head. He had a dried-out look, like he had just stepped out of aggressive chemotherapy. He was driving a newer model red Ford Explorer. Although Widow hadn't planned on heading farther north, not into what looked like blizzard weather, he couldn't complain about the ride. Sometimes he would just change course, go toward other people. A free ride was a free ride.

The old guy wasn't much of a talker, but he seemed nice enough. And talking wasn't something Widow was interested in. He liked the quiet. But most people who picked him up expected conversation. Perhaps that was why a lot of them stopped.

The red Explorer had big white magnetic signs stuck to the doors that read "Dale's Supply Runs." The guy driving wasn't Dale, though. His name was Floyd, and he told Widow he drove across the state line into Wyoming once a month in order to trade with the Lakota Indians on the Red Rain Reservation. Widow hadn't corrected him and said "Lakota Native Americans." What would have been the point? He didn't want to insult the guy who was giving him a ride and driving him about a hundred miles.

Floyd finally broke the silence and said, "So why're you headed into Yellowstone?"

Widow said, "I'm going wherever."

"So, are you like—a drifter?"

Widow nodded.

"Maybe I shouldn't have picked you up then?"

Widow said, "I'm not dangerous. But certainly hitchhiking has gotten a bad reputation these days. Which makes it harder and harder to get rides."

"That's why I picked you up—no harm in giving a young guy a ride. Even if you are a drifter, I give people rides through here all the time. I find it safe enough."

"Well, I sure appreciate it," Widow said, which had a double meaning that the old guy didn't pick up on. On the one hand, Widow was glad for the ride, and on the other, he was thanking Floyd for referring to him as a young guy.

Widow was turning thirty-four at the end of the month, and he didn't feel young.

Floyd said, "You're a nice guy. Why're you drifting? Running away from something?"

Widow stayed quiet, and Floyd seemed to reconsider his comments, and then he said, "I'm sorry. I didn't mean to be nosy."

Widow said, "It's okay. Perfectly reasonable question. No, nothing like that. I just like it."

"Why?"

"It's like a way of life. Open road. Nothing's ever required of me. No responsibilities. No attachments."

"You don't like attachments?"

"For me, they're more like anchors. I feel they weigh me down."

"What about women?"

"What about them?" Widow asked.

Floyd smiled, a good, friendly smile that shined through his beard. Then he said, "Don't you like 'em?"

Widow stayed quiet.

Floyd asked, "Are you gay or something? I don't have a problem with that. Nothing wrong with it."

Widow smiled and then said, "No, I'm not gay. I love women; I just don't want to settle down."

Floyd said, "Well, I can't blame ya. Women are trouble. I gotta wife."

Widow nodded.

"I love her, though. But boy, I can get why you wouldn't want to settle down. You probably have a different woman in every new place you go to?"

Widow thought of Farrah, smiled, and said, "Sometimes."

Floyd let out a hardy laugh that almost turned into a coughing hysteria.

"You okay?"

"Oh yeah. Just remembering what life was like when I was a young buck."

Widow said, "You like this drive?"

"I do." Floyd seemed to sense it was time for a subject change, and he asked, "So you ever been on an Indian reservation before?"

"Can't say that I have. I guess the closest I've ever been to one is passing through the same county."

"Ahh. They're great. They're all different but basically the same. They're kind of sad if you think too much on it. But mostly, they've got an Old West feel. This one we're headed to is about as untouched by society as can be. But they depend on tourism, and that's primarily their only outside source of income. Many others around the country have casinos. This one doesn't."

Widow nodded along and stayed quiet. He thought about it and realized he had never given Indian reservations much thought before. He loved history, so he wasn't really sure why he'd never considered visiting one. It had simply never occurred to him.

Floyd paused and glanced in his side mirror. He switched on his turn signal and changed lanes over to the fast lane. He sped up, and the Explorer revved and jumped. It had a well-oiled engine, no doubt about that.

Widow asked, "So what makes this one so indifferent to society?"

"The Red Rain Reservation doesn't have a casino, like I said, but they rely on tourism and almost have no choice but to stay open for tourists because it's located high in the mountains in Yellowstone National Park."

"An Indian reservation high in the mountains in one of the biggest parks in the world? That sounds really interesting. I can't wait to see it."

"It's quite something. The other thing about it—like a lot of reservations—is that it has a poor side. There're some decent buildings, but most of the residents live in poor conditions," Floyd said.

Widow nodded and said nothing about it. Silence fell between them, and Widow stared out the window.

"I'll tell you something interesting," Floyd said. "Have you ever heard of Red Cloud?"

Widow paused for a moment and thought about it before he answered. Then he said, "Chief Red Cloud was chief of the Oglala Lakota Tribe from 1868 to 1909. He's revered as a powerful war leader. He was one of the most adept Native American opponents the US Army ever faced. In 1866, 1867, and 1868, he waged a successful war campaign known as Red Cloud's War. It was a dispute over the Powder River Country in Northeast Wyoming and part of southern Montana."

Floyd turned his head and stared at Widow for so long that he almost veered over into oncoming traffic. Then he jumped back to life and straightened out the Explorer. He moved his weathered hands to the ten and two o'clock positions on the steering wheel, and then he gazed back at Widow. Just a quick glance this time, not more than a few seconds. He asked, "How did you know all that?"

Widow turned in his seat, and the seat belt pulled with him. He shrugged and said, "I like history. Especially American history. I remember things like that."

Floyd asked, "What do you have, a photographic memory or something?"

"Nothing like that. It's more like I remember useless information. I got a pretty good memory."

Floyd smiled and chuckled a little, probably because he didn't know what else to say to that. Then he said, "Well, your memory will fade as you get older. Trust me. I can barely remember what day it is when I wake up in the morning. Sometimes Mrs. Floyd has to remind me."

Widow smiled and let out a friendly laugh. But he thought his memory wasn't likely to fade because a lifetime of undercover work had taught him to remember details. The little details had saved his life more than once.

Widow rubbed his fingers through his cropped hair, warming his head.

Floyd said, "Old Red Cloud has a descendant at Red Rain. The tribal police comprise two peace officers during the winter months and five in the summer when they add three more deputies. The two officers are father and daughter, and their last name is Red Cloud."

"A father and daughter pair of cops?"

"Yeah. Pretty cool, huh?"

Widow nodded.

"They don't get a lot of cases up there, anyway. I think the biggest crime to happen up there are missing hikers. Which happens every winter or so."

"Missing hikers? What, because of the cold?"

"Of course. The winters are brutal. People go hiking one day, then the next thing you know, there's a blizzard. One second you're having a good time, and the next, you're stranded or worse, buried under twenty feet of snow."

Widow stayed quiet.

"They always find the poor bastards. Some of them get lucky. Some don't."

Silence for several minutes.

Widow glanced over at Floyd and asked, "So what kinds of goods do you deliver to the reservation?"

Floyd said, "Dale sells all kinds of things, but the thing we deliver the most is coffee."

Widow smiled. He loved coffee. "Coffee?"

"Well, coffee beans. We bring huge sacks of them every month. I got a pile of sacks stacked in the cargo space."

Widow turned and sniffed the air.

How did I miss that? He thought. The air was filled with the scent of fresh coffee beans. Coffee was something he couldn't live without. On the road, it had become his best friend.

"Do you drink coffee?" Floyd asked.

"You got no idea," Widow said.

Driving through Yellowstone National Park was one of the best experiences Widow had in six months. The park was enormous and filled with rugged snowcapped mountains, miles and miles, of untouched wilderness, winding roads, and rolling half-green and half-snowy plains as far as the eye could see. He had seen a herd of buffalo roaming in the distance around one of the bends. The closest he had ever been to a buffalo before that was seeing it on a menu.

The traffic that traveled along Highway 20 had weakened miles back. Widow thought he had seen a sign showing that Highway 20 had turned into Grand Loop Road, but he'd paid little attention to the signs. The grandeur of the surrounding forest overcame them. Nature's creations were far more beautiful.

They drove on for a while, following the road as it looped and snaked, and Widow figured out pretty quickly why it was called Grand Loop Road. "Grand" was an understatement, and the loop was more like unending twists and turns, but in the end, it was worth it to follow the road just to take in the scenery.

Widow craned his neck and peered up at the sky. The sun was half-hidden behind a cloud in the three o'clock position. He scanned the horizon. The clouds in the distance were high in the mountains. They seemed to foretell of an incoming storm.

Floyd leaned forward and looked out of the windshield to peer up at the clouds. He said, "Boy, those clouds don't look good."

Widow nodded in agreement.

Floyd returned his eyes to the road and asked, "Do you want me to drop you off at Tower Junction? It'll be much easier to find shelter and even get a ride from there over to Red Rain."

"I'll get out at the reservation. It sounds interesting, and I'm a guy looking to experience interesting things."

"Kid, the reservation is beautiful, and the people there are warm, but they don't really like outsiders who aren't there to trade or buy from them."

"It's not illegal to be there as a tourist, right? This is America."

Floyd said, "No, not exactly. They can't keep you out. At least I don't think they can. But look, there's a shuttle service that runs to Tower Junction. I think it runs until 8 p.m. If I were you, I'd make sure you're on it. There's nowhere to rent a room on the reservation, not like a motel or anything."

The guy paused a beat, then he said, "They'll probably be pretty friendly to you until nightfall. And then they're going to wonder why you're there. So if that's where you want to go, no big deal. But like I said, be on the last shuttle out around nightfall. Tower Junction is a good thirty miles down the road. The last thing that you want is to get stuck hitching rides out there, especially since I'm guessing that those clouds are bringing snow. Maybe worse." Floyd paused again, and then he said, "We should turn on the radio. Check for a weather forecast."

He switched the radio on. The Ford was a newer model vehicle. Widow wasn't sure about the year, but it had all the bells and whistles, including buttons to control the stereo from the steering wheel.

Floyd pressed some buttons and tuned the stereo to a nearby channel that Widow wasn't familiar with. The broadcast came on with one of those buzzing emergency sounds, and then a voice said, "This is an emergency notification of the emergency broadcasting system of Wyoming. As of 2:30 p.m., a blizzard warning is in effect for all of Northern Wyoming. The storm appears to be headed north into Montana. But it could change direction and head into the Yellowstone National Park area. Extreme caution is advised."

Floyd said, "See, that blizzard might sweep through here, and then you'll end up landlocked. Be careful out here on your own."

Widow stayed quiet.

They drove on through the hills and plains and then followed the road as it wound up through the mountains. As they climbed to a higher altitude, Widow could feel the temperature outside dropping dramatically. At one point, Floyd had to blast the heat at the highest setting just to keep the inside of the cabin comfortable.

The road went up over a steep hill, and as they passed over the top, Widow saw straight down into a deep valley outside the passenger side window. It was a fall that would certainly kill him if he opened the door and jumped out, which was not a temptation he had.

At the top of the hill, Grand Loop Road went on to the east, but Floyd slowed the vehicle and pulled over to turn onto a rock and gravel road. The Explorer took to it like an SUV was supposed to. They followed the track, which snaked up through more mountains, and came into a light snowfall. It delighted Widow because he liked the snow. It had been a while since he was stationed anywhere with snow.

And he was from the South, where it never snowed. He remembered it snowing once, way back on New Year's Day when he was a kid, but even that was gone soon after it hit the ground. He remembered his mother letting him make snowballs, which were more like snow cones, but he loved it. They had a snowball fight in the backyard, and she had let him practice his aim.

She had said, "Throw it like it's a live grenade. Don't count. Don't think about it. Let it be second nature. Throw it."

Which had made Widow wonder when he would ever need to throw a live grenade? Of course he had never imagined he'd be in the Navy and actually have to throw live grenades—intending to kill enemies with them.

They drove farther into the mountains, and the air whitened as the wind carried moisture with it. The road ahead curved, and even though things were graying together in a way that was the opposite of the beautiful landscape farther down the mountains, Widow could see well enough.

On the ride up with Floyd, he wondered why they would build a reservation high in the mountains when there was so much land below. Surely, the plains and wilderness and springs below the mountain range provided a much more plentiful place to support an entire tribe of people. But then again, Widow had no idea how Indian reservations had been created. Maybe they were born from a shady treaty with the government. Probably they were formed after months and months of deliberations. He did not know how much say the Native American tribes had in the negotiation process.

The track was a rocky two-lane drive. At first, there were close leafless trees with snow drizzled across the branches. Then they drove on for about a mile, passing open plains, and arriving at a treacherous gorge with a cement bridge that was in decent shape, better than the road. They crossed over the bridge and drove on another half mile before arriving at the entrance to the Red Rain Reservation. Widow sat up higher in his seat and gazed over the

Native American reservation. It was spectacular in an Old West sort of way, like it had been built for the set of a movie. A light smoke trickled up out of the smokestack of a large two-story building that looked like some sort of community center or welcome center that was built close to the reservation entrance.

Before they entered, they came to a set of impressive gates, built high out of thick wood, some kind of oak. They weren't painted and still had that wooden glimmer to them, as if they had been sanded and shined. The sign was written in bold black letters across a flat board. It was almost as if it had been written in the Old West, except that the font was machine-generated. It was a three-tiered sign. The bottom two pieces read, "Red Rain" and "Indian Reservation." The top tier had been broken off and hung vertically from one splintered corner.

Widow craned his neck and followed the sign as they passed beneath it. He turned back to the front when it was behind them and looked back at it in the side mirror. The top tier had read, "Welcome." Someone or something had bowed that part of the sign down, and the locals had never fixed it.

The Explorer's suspension rocked up and down slightly over the snowy track. Floyd drove past the community center. The smoke from the chimney rose into the air, and Widow watched it in the side mirror as they drove farther up. After about another half mile, they came to what appeared to be the bulk of the reservation's civilization. Widow hadn't known exactly what to expect. The traditional economy of reservations wasn't lucrative, but he had never set foot on an Indian reservation before, so it was all new to him. He didn't want to make any prejudgments.

Set off to the west and north were dozens of old, beat-up mobile homes huddled together like a shantytown. There was no logic or reason to the borders between them. Some were parked close enough together to be touching, and some were scattered far apart.

To the east were three separate tracks that broke away from the main one and veered off in three different directions, like a trident with three twisted, uneven tips that speared off into strange directions.

Near the southernmost track, there was a set of low, roughly made stucco buildings, painted in an ugly mix of white and salmon colors. The roofs were flat. Small patches of snow fell off the sides like sand in an hourglass. The ground around the buildings was covered in snow, and Widow could see icy spears of grass piercing through and leaning over to one side. Some of the green blades had cracked and broken off under the weight of the ice.

Everywhere there hung sharp, jagged icicles, like knives hanging from a rack in someone's kitchen. They hung from the sides of the group of buildings and off the broken porches of the mobile homes.

Floyd pulled up closer to the stucco buildings and parked in a space between two old '80s model trucks.

"This is my stop. This first building here is the local store, which has no name really, but everyone calls it the general store. The owner buys a bunch of stuff from us every month. We've been delivering to them for over a decade," Floyd said. He killed the engine and clicked his seat belt loose. It retracted up and back to its starting position.

Widow got out after him. The truck rocked back up on its suspension as he dismounted and shifted his weight to the ground. Widow frowned and shut the door, looking down at Floyd over the roof. He placed one of his hands on the roof and felt the ice-cold steel chill his skin. He said, "Do you need any help bringing the supplies in?"

Floyd looked back up over the roof at him. He studied Widow, looking him up and down like he was seeing him for the first time, even though he had seen him walking on the side of the road. He thought for a moment. The gusts of breath exhaled from his nostrils, and his beard stiffened and froze in the breeze.

He said, "Sure, that'd be fantastic. You mind lifting some of those sacks of coffee beans for me and bringing them inside? They're heavy, but I'm sure you can manage. The Indians here love coffee."

Widow nodded.

Floyd said, "If you want to bring those in for me, we'll call it even for the ride."

Widow shrugged and nodded again. Lug a few big sacks filled with coffee beans a few yards for miles and miles? It sounded like a great deal to him. So he went around to the back of the Explorer and grabbed the handle and opened the door. He stood back as the door rose slowly and automatically. A whiff of the warm air from inside the cabin engulfed his face, and he stopped and stared. Floyd hadn't been lying when he said the sacks were heavy. Before him, there were five huge sacks of coffee beans, all the size of Widow's torso.

He shrugged at the industrial-sized sacks as if he were speaking to them and then reached down and picked up two. The label of the company, "Grinded Coffee Bean Co," was printed along the sides of the bags in a diagonal direction.

He had never heard of Grinded Coffee Bean Co.

The bags were closed and probably sealed, but the aroma of fresh coffee spilled out and filled his nose, rejuvenating him like a contact high. If Widow was honest with himself, he wasn't certain whether the aroma of the beans had really seeped out of the bags or whether just knowing that the coffee beans were that close to him had excited his brain. After all, the bags were probably airtight.

The first bag lumped up in his hands like a beanbag. He hefted two of the gigantic bags up and out of the back of the Explorer and tossed them over his shoulders. They were heavy. He wondered how the old guy carried them on his own. He must've done one bag at a time, or maybe there was a dolly inside the store.

Floyd said, "Walk on in with them. You can leave them up against the wall. And again, I sure appreciate the help."

Widow stayed quiet and followed the instructions. He walked across the snow-covered ground and stepped up a couple of wooden steps that creaked under his weight.

The general store on the outside blended in with the other buildings. It was attached like they had originally been a part of one extensive structure.

Widow prepared to lay one bag down by the door for a second so that he could pull the door open and enter, but right before he started this plan, the door swung open, and a giant Native American stepped out onto the porch. He wore a clean, starched brown apron and black cargo pants with a thick white sweater—wool.

The guy was a native, no doubt about it, because he looked just like a stereotypical Indian from an old Western—like one of those Sergio Leone films. If it weren't for his clothes, Widow would've assumed he was acting in one right now. The guy had long, black hair like a Native American warrior and wore a headband that pulled it back out of his face. The only things the guy was missing were feathers and a bow.

Widow smiled at him and waited as the man stepped aside and held open the door. Then Widow walked past the guy and into the store. Once inside, he put down the bags. Then he turned and looked around, scanning everything. The inside was just as plain as the outside, only slightly more modern. Everything was arranged neatly in a way that made perfect sense—newsstand off to one corner, milk in the coolers in the back, knickknacks on shelves near the front of the store set up as impulse buys.

The store was an average size and average-looking. There were no signs hung up to show what aisles had with what items. There were no candy machines, no soda or snack machines, no carts at the front. Instead, there was a stack of handheld green baskets with no markings.

Widow turned around and walked through the door and back out into the cold air. He moved past the big guy in the apron and walked back toward the Explorer. Where he saw Floyd stepping out from the back of the SUV, carrying one bag of the coffee beans and a few other smaller items in his free hand. He wasn't carrying the bag on his shoulder, as Widow had done. It was more like he was dragging it. When he saw Widow coming toward him, he picked up both his pace and the bag like he didn't want him to think he was weak. Widow had seen that move many times before. Men were always showing up their strength like they had something to prove. He ignored it.

He walked to the back of the Explorer and ducked inside to grab the last two bags. He walked back past the big Native American in the apron. The man didn't smile but looked Widow up and then down, like he was looking for a puzzle piece that was hidden somewhere on Widow's person.

Widow ignored the gesture, walked into the store, and set the two bags next to the first two he had brought in. Looking over the shelves, he saw Floyd walking to the back of the store.

Widow called out to him and said, "I'm going to head out now. Thanks again for the ride."

Floyd said, "Thanks so much for the help. I appreciate it. And good luck to you, son."

Widow stayed quiet and walked out of the store. He passed the big guy one last time and gave him the hat-tipping gesture he had seen in old cowboy movies, even though he had no hat on. Then he carried on, walking back down the road a bit to the station or community center or whatever it was. He figured that since it had been the nicest building so far, and also the first, then it must be where tourists were greeted when they first walked onto the reservation. Therefore, they might have a map of the land. And since he had never heard of Red Rain Reservation before, he figured it would be helpful to take a glance at a map, learn the layout, especially when he looked up at the sky and saw that the sun was barely peeking out through the whiteness. It worried him because the weather report had mentioned a blizzard, and judging by the clouds on the horizon and across the sky, there was something harsh coming this way. Widow figured that knowing the layout of the land was a good idea. He wasn't above sleeping outside, under the stars. But he hoped there would be stars out tonight and not just hard snow and the white squalls of wind. Mountain winters were like that.

He followed the smoke from the chimney he had seen earlier, and it led him back toward the community center. The building was much nicer than the general store complex and far nicer than the shantytown of mobile homes across the road.

Widow walked back over some hills and across the snowy ground. Back at the community center, he stepped onto a blanket of hard snow and then realized there was concrete underneath. The snow had camouflaged the parking lot. He walked through the empty lot and over to the community center. When he got closer, he saw a metal sign on the wall: "Red Rain Tribal Police Around Side."

Widow peered around the side of the building and saw another parking lot with one squad car in it: an Old Crown Victoria covered in snow with the words "Red Rain Reservation Police" faded across the doors. The tires were buried in snow. Next to the one car, he saw tire tracks in the snow that led out of the lot and over to a small one-lane road. The tracks led off toward the mountains to the north.

Widow tried the doors to the community center. They were locked, but there was an office door that was separate. He opened it and walked in. A blast of heat from the office caressed his face. The office was quiet except for an instrumental melody playing from a radio set to a low volume. The radio was an old gray thing with one big speaker and a handle on the top. There was an antenna that extended outward at the one o'clock position, and the tip was broken off, leaving a vicious-looking point at the end.

A woman sat behind the desk. She had long black hair and tan, leathery skin, yet she had a beautiful glow about her that matched the positive vibe she gave off. She wore a purple turtleneck sweater with a design on it that looked like a drawing of a large moon with green grass growing out of it. It was one of the ugliest things Widow had ever seen, but he didn't acknowledge it so as not to offend her— for all he knew, it represented something special to her.

A cheerful smile spread across the woman's face when she saw him, as if she hadn't seen another person all day.

She remained seated and stared up at Widow's hulking bulk standing before her in the tiny office space. Even though she was smiling warmly, Widow could tell she hadn't expected a visitor to come walking into her space. Now that he was standing there, he realized that she had only smiled at his entrance out of habit, because a quick burst of fear seemed to sweep through her eyes and across her face. It was quick. She returned to her cheery smile fast. But Widow had seen it, because he had long ago learned to recognize when people were terrified of him. In fact, he expected it as if it were as natural as breathing, which in a way it was, because the four things very basic to almost every creature on earth were breathing, breeding, feeding, and self-preservation.

And when people met him for the first time, their brains skipped the first three things and focused only on self-preservation. The small, prehistoric parts way in the back of their brains kicked into gear, signaling caution to every one of their appendages. The transcript for this signal read something like: *This is a predator that can hurt you.*

But the civilized part of this woman's brain overrode her instinctive warnings and told her Widow wasn't there to hurt her.

Widow smiled back at her and said, "I need help."

She said, "You came to the right place. Welcome to Red Rain Native American Reservation. What can I do for you?"

"I'm looking for a map. I'm a tourist."

The woman's smile fell a little, and then she said, "On the wall behind you. There's also a small one in the top draw there if you need it."

She pointed to a thin, flat set of drawers in the corner.

Widow raised his hand and said, "Not necessary. I'll glance over the big one and then be on my way and out of your hair."

Widow turned and walked to the map on the wall and looked it over. He traced the roads with his eyes and followed the main one from the entrance through the populated part of the reservation, which was the shantytown, and then he studied the other roads that branched off in multiple directions like tree branches. The routes set into his mind like an internal GPS. He looked over the reservation and saw that it was mostly rugged, mountainous terrain to the west and north and that most of the population was settled in the south, where he was.

Floyd had told him the reservation depended on tourism and outsiders for almost their entire revenue. But looking over the map, Widow had seen little that was geared toward tourism. Sightseeing here would mostly be gazing at nature. There had been no historical battles fought on the land, and there were no memorials or Native American museums that were clearly marked. Most of the so-called tourists must've been people who had already seen Yellowstone Park and wanted to include some Native American history in their adventures, but they would be disappointed in Red Rain Reservation. Widow figured that for him, like many tourists who had wandered onto the reservation seeking some actual sights, this would also turn into a short expedition.

He turned back to the woman behind the desk. Hoping she might have better insight than Floyd, he asked, "Is there anywhere to stay the night in town?"

She smiled at him and said, "Unfortunately, the nearest town is Tower Junction to the southeast. They have a couple of motels there, but we don't have any here. You might rent a room for the night at the general store from Henry Little, who runs the whole operation. He's a nice enough guy. He'll probably rent to you if you wait late enough to ask."

Widow stayed quiet.

The woman asked, "Are you driving?"

Widow said, "No car."

She said, "You should be on the last bus into Tower Junction. If you miss it, head over to the general store and purchase something from Henry, then ask him about a room. Tell him you missed the bus. He's a big man like you. You can't miss him."

Widow nodded. She must've been talking about the huge Native American he had seen at the store already.

Henry Little is an ironic name for a giant, he thought. *Should be Henry the Huge.*

"Thank you for your help," Widow said. He didn't wait for a response. He just turned and left.

5

WALKING ALONE WAS something Widow had done for more than six months now. He was used to it. There was no conflict about it in his head—no internal struggle. Moving on was easy when you kept yourself free and clear of attachments, and that came easily to him since the only person he'd ever been attached to was gone.

Widow had spent the last two hours walking the reservation. He'd pulled up the map in his head and had followed it along the main road, venturing off the beaten path twice and discovering exactly what he had already predicted—most of the sights to see on the reservation weren't man-made. He had seen thick forests, incredible mountains with tremendous peaks in the distance, the old western-style houses and structures of the wealthier residents, and even some wild animals—and all of it was covered in snow. Widow was awed by the natural beauty of the land and disappointed in the low care given to most of the public buildings.

As Floyd had said, most citizens were poor.

Widow didn't want to speculate, but he imagined it was related to government taxes, no economic viability, or all of the above. The one thing he had learned so far was that the reservation had some tourism flowing into it, but the locals didn't seem too keen on tourists. Therefore, they built no monuments or attractions for tourists to visit.

Reviewing the general store in his mind, Widow could perfectly recall the layout. There were some items targeted at tourists, most of which were the knickknacks that lined the walls near the entrance. Widow guessed that Henry Little's place was the only game in town, so to speak. Business didn't appear to be booming at the general store, but then again, the current weather wasn't ideal for tourists. Maybe tourism on the reservation picked up in the summer months. It was too bad the Natives hadn't opened a ski resort or casino near any of the mountains on their property. The skiing would probably be incredible. And Floyd had said that many Native American reservations had embraced casinos, and they had proven to be profitable for their respective communities.

The Red Rain residents didn't seem as open to growing their economic status through such endeavors. Perhaps they were too proud, or perhaps they viewed it as selling out. Widow wasn't sure, mainly because—aside from the woman in the community center—no one had really spoken to him. The entire time he'd been walking, he hadn't seen another soul. Not a car passed on the roads. Not a single resident had come out of his home.

Widow looked up at the sun in the sky and figured the time was near what his mind had calculated. It was 4:51 p.m. He looked to the western horizon and watched the encroaching peach, pink, and violet colors of the sky as the sun set over the mountains.

Remembering Floyd's warning about being stuck on the reservation for the night, he returned to the primary area near the stucco buildings, the community center, and the general store. He thought the shuttle headed to Tower Junction was probably doing its last runs for the night. Floyd had said the last one was at 8 p.m., but judging by the weather on the horizon, he thought it best to head back sooner. He had seen all there was to see in Red Rain.

At least that was what he thought.

6

Widow walked back to the central hub of the reservation in sixteen minutes flat. He hadn't explored its entirety—it was too big to explore completely in two hours—but he had seen enough and was ready to move on. So far, there had been nothing special about Red Rain Reservation except for the majestic scenery, which he could've seen by staying in Yellowstone National Park. The only other thing he had noticed was that the inhabitants of the reservation were less than friendly, but frankly, they weren't that interesting to him.

But all that was about to change in thirty-six seconds. Widow turned around the back corner of one of the buildings, attached to the general store, and walked along the wall until he turned another corner. And that was when he witnessed an unsettling scene.

Three people. Two men and one police officer. The two men wore street clothes—brown jackets, dark cargo pants, combat boots. One had a white shirt under his jacket, and the other wore a black button-down shirt with a crooked collar. No tie. They both had buzz cuts like his own. He figured the odds were good that these guys were also ex-military. The way they stood and crowded up on the officer was a military-trained move—no doubt in Widow's mind about that.

The guy in the black shirt was doing all the talking. The guy in the white was shoving the officer with one big, gloved hand. Widow witnessed the whole thing. The two guys had the officer literally back into a corner near the back of the general store.

The officer was a woman—young, Native American features, and stunning. She had thick, long black hair braided into a fishtail. She didn't speak, but was obviously in distress. Widow wondered why she didn't pull out her service weapon. He could see the handle of a pristine Glock 22 Gen4 holstered down by her side. The back strap allowed the user to adjust the grip to fit smaller and larger hands alike. The rough design and the hard, black color glimmered in the dying sunlight.

Widow had helped a woman in distress more than once. But the last time had been back in Black Rock, Mississippi. A cop had been harassing a local woman. Widow had intervened and disrupted the harassment, as a gentleman should, which was something his mother had instilled in him. She had taught him early on that there were gentlemen, and there were ladies, and then there were other people. These two guys were obviously *other* people.

Widow clenched his fists and rolled his sleeves up to his biceps. He looked the two guys up and down, and then he noticed that the guy in the black shirt with the crooked collar had a bulge in the back of his brown jacket. It had to be a gun tucked into his waistband. Widow assumed the other guy also had a gun on him, and he reevaluated his approach in his mind. His brain worked like a computer, evaluating scenarios and outcomes, trying to figure out the best approach to take.

Widow's brain analyzed the situation much like one of those machines from the *Terminator* movies—delivering real-time battlefield awareness and feedback so that his mind could quickly assess and plan the right course of action to neutralize the bad guys. His brain factored in the weather —the wind, the snow, and the dwindling light from the setting sun to the west. And the icicles that hung like stalactites from the corner of the building above them.

In the end, Widow decided it best to use the good old element of surprise.

He looked over his shoulder and was pleased to see that the sun was setting directly behind him. The setting light was decreasing, but it was sharp and crisp and shot out across the sky like a laser beam. He crept down low so that the laser beams of sunlight swept over his body to blind anyone looking in his direction. Not even the officer could've seen him until he was already on them. He crept carefully past the wall of the closest building and saw his shadow directly out in front of him on the ground. He adjusted his trajectory, so the shadow shrank in size, and he continued to move toward them.

His new shoes were comfortable and silent—two advantages he appreciated at that moment because they enabled a guy of his size to sneak up behind two ex-military trained men. Widow was not a naturally stealthy kind of guy, but even though he wasn't what most would call graceful, he could still be silent when he needed to be. In his old job, he'd needed to be stealthy many times.

The time from when he had seen the two guys until he was down low and only three feet behind them was exactly twelve seconds—a record in his mind. He smiled because he hadn't lost it as much as he had thought. But then something else happened. It wasn't a mistake on his part that got him caught at the last second. Not entirely.

As he neared the backs of the two guys, he rose out of his crouch and saw an expression of what he could only describe as sheer horror sweep across the police officer's face.

Widow stood behind them, rising so that he towered over them. The Native American cop couldn't see his face or his skin color. The only thing she had seen in that second was his size. In a microsecond, her face—a face that only moments ago Widow had thought was the most beautiful face he had ever seen—morphed into the face of someone who had looked into the depths of evil. And it was that expression that gave his presence away to the men.

Widow hadn't identified which of the two guys was the leader or the faster one to react or the deadlier one, but at that moment, he learned it was the guy in the crooked-collared, black shirt because he spun around and went for his gun. Tucking a gun in the rear of your waistband has both advantages and drawbacks. It feels natural and more comfortable than tucking it into the front and is a lot less deadly to a man's vital areas in case of the gun accidentally firing. It's also easier to conceal from people who are in front of you. However, a huge drawback is that it's slower to pull, especially when there's a guy directly behind you.

In two moves, Widow reached out with his left hand and clamped it down on the guy's right elbow, which was bent back because he was reaching behind him to pull his gun out. Next, Widow reared back and then lunged forward in a powerful headbutt that started on the heels of his feet and launched upward.

His head whipped forward and crashed into the bridge of the guy's nose, and there was a loud *crack!*

The blow was powerful, but not Widow's best work, which wasn't because he had gotten weaker since leaving NCIS. He simply didn't want to kill the guy. He only wanted him out of commission as fast as possible, and a perfectly delivered headbutt would do the job. And it did, because the guy collapsed forward to his knees and grabbed his nose with his free hand. His nose was broken in at least two places. The guy had also dropped his gun, and it plopped down into the snow with a light thud.

Widow let go of the guy's right arm and directed his focus to the other guy in the white shirt. The sunlight was still bright enough to keep the guy blinded. He could tell because he had stepped aside and saw the guy's face light up like a spotlight had been shined directly onto it. He had been quick to react. Faster than Widow had thought because he had already drawn his gun, but it was pointed downward, into the snow—probably so he wouldn't accidentally shoot his friend.

The guy in the white shirt had apparently leaned toward the side of caution, as he had been trained to do, but

Widow didn't have that same programming. His nature and his training told him to act, not threaten. *React first.* To most people, a drawn gun was enough of a threat to stop them cold, even if it was pointed down, but not to Widow. To him, a drawn gun was a problem quickly resolved with quick action.

The guy in the white shirt squinted his eyes like he was trying to identify whether he was being attacked by an enormous creature or a man. But he never got the chance to confirm because Widow stepped left, lunged forward, and cracked the guy right in the middle of his chest. It was a perfect blow.

It happened so fast that even without the sunlight blinding her, the police officer wouldn't have even seen it. She would've only witnessed a couple of quick jerks of Widow's right shoulder. A jerk forward. A jerk backward. Like a shot fired from a captive bolt gun, used by ranchers and in slaughterhouses to knock out the cattle before they're slaughtered. It's called stunning. The gun is loaded with a single retractable bolt with a sharp piercing tip. The bolt fires and is propelled by pressurized air or a blank cartridge. It penetrates the skull of the animal, enters the cranium, and calamitously damages the cerebrum. Because of the destruction of vital centers of the brain and an increase in intracranial pressure, the animal loses consciousness—it's stunned.

Widow stunned the guy in the white shirt.

The guy dropped his gun, and it fell and half-sank down into the snow. Simultaneously, he flew back off his feet like he had been hit in the chest by a shotgun blast. He, too, half-sank deep into the snow. His head fell back and didn't come back up. He was unconscious.

Widow stepped forward and checked both. The guy in the crooked collar was still wriggling around on the ground, cupping his nose. Not an immediate threat. Widow walked over to the other guy. He knelt and lifted the guy's head up and out of the snow. It was clear he was still alive because little puffs of air came out of his nose like vapor. He was breathing fine.

Widow gently laid the guy's head back down in the snow, face-up so he could breathe, and stepped back up. He hadn't really thought about how the cop would react to his interfering. He hadn't expected her to be grateful, not necessarily, but a thank-you would be nice. Not what he got. What he got was completely unexpected.

Upright, in a trained stance with a look of fear and confusion on her face, was the cop he had just helped. In her hands was her Glock 22 Gen4. It was out, aimed, and pointed straight up—at the two o'clock position because of the height difference—at Widow's face.

She said, "Don't move, or I'll shoot."

7

Cops are taught to use what's called "the cop voice." A loud, fearsome tone. Sharp, precise commands. And most of all, an authoritative voice. *"Get on the ground!"* or *"Freeze!"* or *"Put your hands up!"* Any variation of commands like that would work. They were trained to show confidence. They were trained to show power, force, and strength. The one thing they were trained not to do was show fear or hesitation. Signs of fear could get you shot. Signs of fear could get you killed.

The police officer Widow had just assisted was pointing a gun at him and saying the right words, but not in the right way. She trembled. Widow could see the fear in her eyes and hear it in her voice.

"Get your hands up!" she shouted. "Get them up! Get them up!"

This upset Widow for two reasons. First, he had just helped her out. Clearly, she had needed help because she was letting these two guys push her around, and assaulting an officer was a crime everywhere. Widow had no doubt about that. Second, he found himself uncontrollably attracted to her. He had noticed how attractive she was from the first moment he had seen her, but it wasn't until now that he could see just how incredible she was.

She had black hair, dark brown eyes, and crisp eyebrows on a smooth forehead. Her cheekbones were high and well-defined, and she had long, thin lips. There was a thin nose that bridged her eyes seamlessly. Her skin was the color of a gently worn saddle. The only thing unattractive about her was the fact that she pointed a gun at him. Maybe he hadn't expected her to be grateful for the help, but it certainly insulted him that now she was trying to detain him after all he'd done to help her. After all, it was the other two guys who had assaulted her, and now she knew they had been carrying concealed weapons, which might've been a crime on this reservation. He wasn't sure.

"Relax. I'm not a threat," Widow said in a firm voice, trying to hide his annoyance at her reaction.

Not a good start, he thought.

She shouted, "Get your hands up!"

Widow slowly raised his hands. Over to his right, he noticed the sunlight was almost gone. If he wanted, he could've jumped right, scrambled to her, and gotten hold of the Glock. He could've pushed it down and to the left and rendered it useless unless she wanted to shoot at the ground. But he discarded this plan because he was a good guy.

No need to assault her, even though she apparently wouldn't have done anything about it, he thought.

He glanced down at her nameplate. It said, "Red Cloud." A look of intrigue splashed across his face, and he thought about Chief Red Cloud from his conversation with Floyd. She must've been related to him, proudly wearing his name as her own.

He glanced a little lower and saw a badge clipped to the front of her belt at the lower right-hand side of her abdomen.

The badge had an Old West design to it. It was natural, unadorned, and simple with a rusty color swirling through it. At the top of the badge was a blackened arrow that faced upward with the name of her tribe plastered across the top in big letters: "Lakota." In the middle of the badge, just under the tribal name, was the seal of Native American head, feathers and all. At the bottom was the word "Police."

Officer Red Cloud cocked her head to the left and stared coldly into Widow's face. She said, "Turn around slowly and keep your hands up till I tell you otherwise."

Widow didn't argue. He shrugged and turned slowly, keeping his arms in the air.

"Lower your arms slowly and place them behind your back."

Not again, Widow thought. He'd been arrested a little over six months ago for beating up three rednecks who had been picking on a weaker guy, and now he was about to be hand-cuffed for the same crime. He thought that maybe he wasn't supposed to help total strangers out anymore. So far, the endeavor had brought him nothing but trouble.

"Are you arresting me?"

"Sir, please comply. Place your arms down behind your back," Officer Red Cloud said.

Shrugging, Widow closed his eyes tight and placed his arms down behind his back, his wrists pressed together. No tightening of his muscles. No intention of resisting. He kept everything loose.

He heard Officer Red Cloud step closer to him in the snow. Her boots crunched down—soft. She moved in closer behind him, never lowering her firearm until she was close enough to grab him. She had dealt with big guys before. It came with the job. She had been trained to do so way back in the Law Enforcement Academy of Wyoming.

The bulk of the school was stationed clear at the opposite corner of the state, in Douglas, Wyoming. But she had attended most of her classes on a university campus in Cody. It was a joint program, a satellite of the academy, but the courses that taught her how to engage a man of Widow's stature were courses she had to take one semester when she moved down to Douglas.

Even though Officer Red Cloud had been properly trained, this guy was different. This guy had just sneaked up behind two men with special ops backgrounds and taken them down faster than any takedown she had ever seen before. He was serious business.

She waited until she was within reaching distance of Widow, and then she lowered her gun, held it out one-handed. She reached behind her and took out a pair of handcuffs. Widow heard the clatter of the metal on metal from the chain and the cuffs.

Officer Red Cloud smashed the first cuff on his left wrist and then the second on his right. She jerked on the chain and made sure they were tight enough to hold him. It was an action she had taken hundreds of times before on both practice and real suspects, but this was the first time she had actually been afraid the steel cuffs wouldn't be enough to restrain Widow.

Widow looked back over his shoulder at her and asked, "Is this how you treat every guy who tries to help you?"

"Help me? How the hell are you helping me?"

Widow stayed quiet, afraid of showing his annoyance with her.

She didn't wait for a response. Instead, she jerked the cuffs and holstered her weapon, but she left the safety snap undone in case she had to draw it again, and Widow noticed.

She tugged on his cuffs like reins on a bridle, and she moved him in a southerly direction, away from the buildings and the two guys.

She stopped ten steps past the guys and barked at Widow, "Stay here. Don't move."

Widow stayed quiet and complied. He felt her let go of the cuffs. He thought, *I could run. I could make it into those trees.* Maybe she'd get one good shot off, but she wouldn't hit him unless she was a crack-shot. No way. The light was almost nonexistent, and Widow was fast—not the fastest runner in the world, but fast enough. He knew he could've been behind the bunch of trees only thirty yards away from him in no time, but he didn't run. He'd done nothing wrong. She was the one in the wrong.

Then he heard Officer Red Cloud speak to the guy with the crooked collar and the broken nose. She said, "That nose is bad. You should tape it up and head back to Tower Junction. Go to the emergency room there." She paused a beat and said, "I'd call you an ambulance, but we don't have one here. Your friend doesn't look so good. I'd take him to a doctor as well. Like I told you, we don't know a Jacobs here. Tell your bosses that and don't come back. We have rights here, gentlemen."

The guy with the broken nose muttered something back to her. Widow couldn't make it out. And if he had broken the law by helping her out, then he was about to break it again by not obeying her. He turned and faced them. He didn't want his back to two guys he had just laid out. Not when he knew they were armed. Why she wasn't doing anything about it. He had no idea.

There was no need for Widow to worry because one guy was still unconscious, and the other guy was cupping his nose. He wouldn't be able to do anything because he was using both of his hands just to keep his nose from bleeding out. *Can a guy die from a nosebleed?* Widow wasn't sure, but he knew if it was possible, it'd be this guy. The surrounding snow was colored crimson red from his blood loss so far.

First time for everything, Widow thought.

The cop turned to Widow and walked back to him. The fear had left her face, replaced by a confidence Widow expected from cops.

She approached him and said, "Face the other way and walk."

Widow obeyed.

They stayed quiet for the next minute as they walked south, and then she pulled him to turn east toward a second road that connected to the other side of the row of buildings. It was a road Widow hadn't walked on, but he recalled it from the map he had memorized. The road snaked north and zigzagged west, eventually connecting to another branch of the tree of roads that ran into the mountains.

They walked some more and then looped around a corner, and Widow saw their destination. It was a parked police cruiser in an empty lot to the southeast. The only way Widow could find the entrance into the lot was by following the tire tracks from the cruiser that led back out. The cop must've just parked there since the time he had arrived on the reservation because it hadn't snowed since he'd been there, and the car didn't have a flake of snow anywhere on it.

They reached the car, and Officer Red Cloud said, "Stop," and "Lean down, face on the car."

She used her small hand to push Widow gently forward against the passenger door of the car. She moved left and opened the door, then stepped back and said, "Get in."

Widow ducked down and got into the rear of the car. She was supposed to push his head down so that he wouldn't hit it getting into the car—a pretty standard universal cop move, like Cop 101—but she didn't do it, and Widow knew why. It was because she couldn't reach his head.

Officer Red Cloud was about five eight, which was tall for a woman. Most of the women Widow had ever met were shorter, but she was still far shorter than he. Eight inches, at least.

Widow sat back on his hands in the back seat and got as comfortable as he could get. He stared forward in a kind of trance. He wasn't angry anymore, but the experience had moved far beyond being funny at this point. Now it was real. He was going to the station, and he was probably going to spend the night behind bars.

Widow always tried to find the good in any situation. Even though he may have looked menacing on the outside, on the inside, he was smiling because he realized that at least now he'd have a room for the night, and he didn't have to pay for it. Probably get a free meal or two out of it. A free room and free food were always a welcome prospect for him. In addition, this was the second night in a row he had a free room for the night, and both had been because of beautiful women—Farrah from Utah and now Officer Red Cloud from Red Rain Reservation—although he'd rather be with Farrah at this point.

Ironic, he thought, and then he thought about that old Tom Hanks movie *Forrest Gump*: "Life is like a box of chocolates." In Widow's case, life was like a box of chocolates—he never knew what he was going to get.

Officer Red Cloud opened the driver's side door and plopped down in the seat. She strapped her seat belt on.

She inserted the keys in the ignition, fired up the engine, revved it up, glanced back at Widow in the rearview, then looked forward again.

Cold air blasted through the vents, and she shivered. She let the car run for a while so the heater would warm up.

Widow leaned forward and asked, "Are you going to tell me why I'm being detained?"

She looked in the rearview mirror. Widow could see her forehead. For her to see his eyes, she had to reach up and adjust the mirror, which she did. She said, "Interfering with police work. Obstruction of justice. Assault on an officer of the law. Take your pick, sir."

"Assault on an officer?"

She said, "Yes."

"What officer? You were the one being assaulted. I helped you."

She turned back in her seat and faced him. Her smooth forehead crinkled violently. She said, "Sir, I'm not the officer you assaulted. Those guys are."

Suddenly and violently and involuntarily, Widow swallowed hard. The two guys poking and prodding and accosting her like that in public hadn't been criminals. They were cops. That's why she hadn't drawn her service weapon.

She must've seen the realization in his eyes because she started nodding, and then she said, "Yeah, that's right. You assaulted two federal agents, and now you're going to jail."

She said nothing else but turned around in her seat, popped the gear into reverse, and hit the gas, accelerating backward. Then she shuffled the lever to drive and hit the accelerator, and the tires peeled out in the snow, spraying a trail of white haze behind the car.

Seconds later, they were driving over the rugged, snow-covered roads back to the police station, and for the first time in months, Widow was worried.

8

FOR THE SECOND time in less than a year, Widow was going to spend the night in jail. And it was his own fault. *Why can't I just mind my own business like an ordinary person?* He thought. *I'm not a cop anymore.*

Officer Red Cloud pulled into the parking lot of the police station at the back of the community center, where Widow had memorized the map of the reservation earlier. The daylight had died away completely, but the northern territory of Wyoming wasn't really pitch black at night because the sky was lit up by billions of bright stars and solar satellites. This night had that kind of skyline, but only to the south and the west. To the north and to the east loomed the clouds, carrying what the old guy, Floyd, had said was probably a blizzard.

Widow sat back on his hands in the police cruiser and waited for Officer Red Cloud to park the car, slide the gear into park, kill the engine, and step out. She shut her door and walked around to Widow's door and popped it open.

Then, in some sort of primitive reaction of self-preservation, she jumped back on her heels and rested one hand on the hilt of her Glock.

She said, "Get out."

Widow leaned forward and stepped out of the car with his head bent down. He barely cleared the doorframe, trying to get out. He stretched as best as he could from his toes to his upper torso. Widow felt ten times better being out of the cramped space in the back seat. He stretched his fingers out behind him, and Officer Red Cloud could hear his knuckles *crack*. It was Widow's way of showing his agitation at being arrested for being a Good Samaritan.

He said, "Where to?"

She said, "Forward."

She pointed straight ahead to a faded orange door with a security camera above it. The door looked more like the back door to a warehouse or a shed or a hardware store than it did a police station. The station itself had no sign—on the door, on the building, or anywhere in the parking lot out front. Widow guessed it didn't need a clear sign, because everyone who mattered probably already knew its location, and everyone who didn't know its location probably didn't matter.

Widow walked toward the door until Officer Red Cloud tugged on his handcuffs again, halting him like he was a horse on reins. He stopped and growled in a low, deep, and primitive caveman grunt he hadn't meant to make, but it came out involuntarily. She must've been startled by it because she paused a beat, again showing he scared her. Then Officer Red Cloud made a fatal mistake—she released her grip on his cuffs and walked past him, past his reach.

Even though he was restrained and couldn't have reached out with his hands and snatched her up, he could've easily lunged forward and head-butted her, like he'd done to the federal agent. He could've killed her. He suspected she knew it.

Officer Red Cloud walked past Widow to the orange door and pulled out her keys. She slid a key into the dead bolt and unlocked the door. Widow thought it to be an outdated security measure, but he wasn't surprised.

She turned back to him and said, "Inside. Follow the line on the floor."

Widow entered the station and saw no reception area— probably because they had entered from the back. Most stations had an entrance for arrests and bookings separate from the public entrance. That wasn't his experience six months ago in Mississippi, but Wyoming was a different state with a different set of practices.

Officer Red Cloud walked behind Widow as he followed the line on the floor, which led him down the corridor and under bright fluorescent lights with hoary, cracked covers. They turned a corner, came into a large room. On one side, Widow saw three sets of holding cells facing the bullpen, which comprised only four cubicles with four chairs, four desks, four lamps, and four computers. The station itself was clean and tidy and plain and efficient. Nothing was out of place or impractical. Everything had a purpose, and everything had a place.

The floor was a white stone tile with copious black borders. The cells were clean, the cleanest Widow had ever seen in a basic jail system—clean toilets, clean beds, clean floors, clean walls, and polished black bars with fallow locks that looked like they were straight off the shelf of a hardware store.

Officer Red Cloud said, "Go over to the first bars. Step inside."

Widow finally broke through his tension and asked, "Are you really going to go through with this? I was trying to help you."

"You attacked two federal agents, and you broke one of their noses! Not to mention that the guy you knocked out might have a concussion or worse! What did you expect would happen?"

"I thought they were harassing you! I'm sorry that they were federal agents or whatever. From where I stood, it looked like you needed help. How was I supposed to know they were cops? Besides, cops or not, those guys were harassing you, and that's a crime no matter if it's done by a civilian or another cop. I know what I'm talking about."

"How's that?"

"I used to be a cop in the Navy."

Officer Red Cloud said, "Well, if you were a cop, you'll recognize the inside of a jail cell. Now get in!"

Widow shrugged and stepped inside the open cell.

Officer Red Cloud left the cuffs on him and slammed the door shut. It was one of those old-time cells where the door opened and swung outward. Not the automatic kind that slid into the wall and was programmed or controlled by a security booth. The lock engaged on impact, making a clicking sound.

Officer Red Cloud said, "Now step backward and slide your hands through the cell bars so I can unlock you."

Widow complied with her instructions. But she didn't unlock him, not yet. Instead, she asked, "Got any weapons in your pockets?"

"No."

Widow had thought it strange that she'd skipped patting him down, but now he knew why. She hadn't wanted to touch him or get too close to him.

She said, "Stand there and wait. I'm going to pat you down."

Widow stood with his back against the cold bars. They chilled him even through his clothes.

Officer Red Cloud kept her fingers loose, and she gently and thoroughly patted down his pockets, his waistband, and his legs, especially near his shoes. Then she stood back up and said, "You're good. I'll unlock you."

She took her keys out again, unlocked him, and then slid the cuffs off his wrists.

Widow cracked his fingers to loosen them up, then rubbed his wrists. His wrists were the size of two-by-fours, and handcuffs were notoriously uncomfortable on them. He turned around slowly. It was the first time she had really gotten a good look at his face.

Officer Red Cloud didn't smile, but there was a slight look on her face. It was a look Widow had seen before. He was no Romeo and definitely no ladies' man. In fact, he was, mostly, socially awkward. Because he had lived undercover for so long, most of his social skills were probably based on lies. Then again, he had always been on the fringe, kind of like a tree in the desert. He didn't fit in with what was normal, and he preferred it that way. One reason he enjoyed wandering and being alone so much was that was where he fit in—out there.

And even though Widow had never been a ladies' man, he had some good luck with women in the recent past. He was becoming more confident in his own skin. It was a lot easier once he let go of all the conditioning of the small-town public schools. In the real world, when you were a stranger everywhere you went, you were always the new kid. The new kid didn't quite fit in anywhere. And that wasn't bad. And not good. It was just different—set apart from everyone else. And he enjoyed being apart from everyone else. His place was no place. His station in life wasn't to settle down. It was to move and to use his talents to help people who couldn't help themselves. He felt good about his good deeds so far, but Widow was far from a saint. He was pretty sure that sainthood required pure thoughts, and at that moment, Officer Red Cloud was filling his head with thoughts of the impure kind. And he had noticed the glimmer that had flitted across her face just then.

He wasn't blind. He knew when a woman liked him. And she was attracted to him, whether or not she wanted to admit it.

Deep down, humans are animals. And in the animal world, men and women could be instantly attracted to each other without explanation, without words, and without admittance. That was the attraction he felt for her, and he assumed it was what she felt for him because, minus that primitive attraction, she wasn't exactly on his good side. After all, she had arrested him for helping her out.

Widow said, "Officer Red Cloud, aren't you going to book me? Fingerprint me? Charge me? Read me my rights? You know, all of that cop stuff."

Red Cloud leered at him, which made Widow think his anger was mutual. He must've interrupted something much more complicated than harassment by two agents in street clothes. It smelled fishy to him, but he no longer cared about the details.

She said, "All in good time. Reservation law says I can detain anyone for any reason for up to forty-eight hours. I'll get back to you on the charges. For now, you just sit tight."

Widow asked, "Aren't you going to ask for my ID? My name? You patted me down, but you never took my possessions."

She stopped, upset, and turned to him. She must have not even thought of that.

"Give it to me."

Widow dug into his pocket and pulled out his passport. He handed it to her through the bars. She stared at it and stuffed it into her right front pocket. Maybe she'd enter him into the system. Maybe not.

She said, "What else you got?"

"You patted me down."

"Don't piss me off! You're already in trouble! What else you got?"

"Toothbrush. Bankcard."

"Keep it," she said, and turned to walk away.

Widow said, "Gotta go to the bathroom."

Officer Red Cloud shrugged and said, "Don't care. Tell it to the walls." She turned again, buckled her gun holster-snap shut, and walked off down the corridor. A moment later, Widow heard the back door open again, and her voice came echoing down the hall. She said, "I'll be back."

The door slammed shut behind her. Widow heard it lock.

He stared into the station, didn't know how to react or what to think. He'd never seen such unprofessional police work in his life. She'd left him locked in a holding cell by himself. No guards. No other prisoners. Life on the reservation was certainly a lot different from what he'd imagined.

Widow tried to find the good in every situation, and he thought again about how he had a room for the night if she kept him locked up overnight, which he'd bet all of his money she would. So at least he had a warm place to sleep. It was better than riding or hiking thirty miles to Tower Junction and spending money on a motel.

Never in his life had he ever met a cop like her, but then again, never in his life had he ever met a woman like her.

9

THE CLOSEST HOSPITAL was in Tower Junction, thirty miles away. It was a four-story building with off-white paint and hunter-green trim, which had been dulled by many harsh winters of snow blasting down from the sky. In the parking lot was one emergency vehicle and one police cruiser, the employees' cars, and a Ford King Ranch painted gray, with thick black tires. The registration in the glove box said it was owned by Carlos George Rodrigo III. It was a Mexican name, but the guy who had been driving Mr. Rodrigo's truck wasn't Mexican. Not by blood. Not by birth. And not even by distant cousins.

The guy who had commandeered the truck and parked it in the hospital's parking lot was a tall man with one fierce blue eye and one grayed-out eye. He had a jagged scar that ran down his face and replaced part of his nose with a tiny triangle-shaped hole.

The man with the scar stood next to the two federal agents in a hospital room. One was bandaged across his face and had a nose splint on a severely broken nose, and the second was awake but staring blankly at his surroundings. One minute, he had been standing facing Amita Red Cloud, the cop from the reservation, and the next minute, he was waking up in a hospital with no memory of the seconds and minutes in between.

The guy with the jagged scar scowled at the two agents with a look they had seen before and feared. He asked, "How many guys attacked the two of you?"

The guy with the broken nose said in a nasal voice, "It was one… one guy."

The guy with the jagged scar said, "One. One?"

"Yes."

The man with the scar turned to look at the other agent and asked, "Did you see him?"

"I don't remember."

The man with scar stayed quiet for a long minute. He looked back over his shoulder at the door to the room. No one entered, and there was a little noise from the outer hallway. No nurses or patients or doctors were walking up and down the halls. He turned back to the two agents and said, "Get up."

"Why?" asked the one with the broken nose.

The guy with the jagged scar pulled out a Kimber Custom Model 1911, a standard .45 ACP, and let his hand fall to his side—the weapon obvious to both agents.

They jumped up out of their beds, and the guy with the broken nose said, "Hold on a second. We're sorry."

The guy with the scar asked, "You said that one guy attacked the two of you. *One* guy?"

"Yes."

"Yeah."

"Was he armed?"

The two agents were standing in the middle of the room, staring at the gun in his hand. They looked at each other, not knowing what to think. They did not know what their boss was going to do. Fear and confusion flashed across their faces.

"Relax. Now answer the question. Was the guy armed?"

"No," said the guy with the broken nose.

"I don't believe it. No way did an unarmed man attack the two of you and get the best of you. Two trained agents of the best intelligence agency and military in the world?" He took his gun and tossed it onto the nearest bed and then turned his body to show the two agents he was unarmed. He moved in closer to the one with the broken nose and said, "Now I'm unarmed, right?"

"Yes, sir," the guy responded.

In a sudden flurry of powerful and skilled blows, the guy with the scar punched the guy with the broken nose.

Once. Twice. In the gut. Once. Twice. Three times in the left rib cage. The agent spilled forward and onto his knees. He screamed, but then he was hit straight in the face—a brutal blow. The agent's nose splint snapped, and shards of metal pierced through the tape on his face. Blood erupted from his wound like a geyser.

Then the guy with the scar looked back at the other agent and said, "Remember that? You got that?"

The agent held up his hands in a defensive position. He said, "No. I'm sorry. We're sorry. The guy must've been specially trained to get the drop on us like that."

"That's the good news. Good for you. That cop looked him up after you two left." He clenched his fists then said, "He's got a completely clean record."

"How's that good?"

"It encouraged me to look beneath the surface, and I found he had a classified record. He's former undercover NCIS. He was deployed with the SEALs. That's why I'm going to let you two idiots off."

The guy with the jagged scar dropped his fists and relaxed. He didn't pound on the other agent but turned, bent down, and popped the other guy twice more in the face—once right in the broken nose and then a second time in the forehead. The guy fell back and was knocked completely unconscious.

The guy with the scar rose back up and glanced over his shoulder at the other agent and said, "Now he's been knocked out too. If you mess up again, the next time, I'll have to even you out with him. I don't think you want a broken nose, not like the one he's got. Now turn him over, so he doesn't drown in his own blood. I'll send the nurse in to reset his nose."

The guy with the scar stopped at the bed, picked up his Kimber Custom 1911 and holstered it, and walked out of the hospital room. The door shut slowly behind him, hissing on its arc to a fully closed position.

10

WIDOW SAT in the jail cell in the freezing temperatures of Northern Wyoming and wondered when the hell he was going to learn his lesson. Most people just minded their own business. But he was always getting into trouble.

Is this what it's like trying to do the right thing? He thought.

The station was completely empty. He could hear the wind howl and the office machines humming and the low, ambient sounds of hibernating computer systems. A fax came in and broke the silence. It was an old dinosaur of a machine. He heard it rev up like a 1970s truck coming back to life. Then he heard a whirring sound and the rolling of paper on an internal track, and then the sound of printing.

Officer Red Cloud had been nice enough to leave the lights on for him. Another silver lining he added to his list of positives about her.

She must like me, he joked to himself.

Widow had spent the last hour lying back on the cot in his cell and staring at the ceiling. He let his mind drift in thought. At one point, he analyzed the different routes he could take once he got out of this cell. He had thought of five of them, all of which branched off from a long stint on Interstate 212 and headed east. East was the heading he had come to Wyoming from, and he didn't plan on changing his course just because of a police officer and her inability to stand up to some federal agents, although he thought that the best thing to do was to take off the first chance he got. Then he thought about how he was going to get out of his current situation. If the cops pressed charges, he'd have to do something he'd really rather not do, which was to skip town. Skipping town on misdemeanors wasn't really a big deal, but skipping out on charges of assaulting a cop—and two federal agents at that—wouldn't be easy, because then Widow would be a fugitive. The agency in question wouldn't just let that go. Even worse was the fact that the two agents probably wouldn't let it go. He was sure they'd take it personally.

Every cop he'd ever known always had.

In fact, he expected a visit from them as soon as they were out of the hospital. Widow hoped they'd accept his apology and thought perhaps he could persuade them to give him a beating instead of charging him with assault—a quid pro quo. He didn't really want to be beaten up by a couple of big ex-military guys with a grudge, but it sounded better than the serious jail time he'd be facing otherwise.

Suddenly, Widow heard a noise from down the corridor beyond the small bullpen, and he sat up on his cot and faced forward. He had an experience once before while in jail that had made him suspicious of unusual sounds coming from hallways.

It sounded like a man making the usual huffing and grunting sounds that men make, someone who thought he was alone—the sounds of a man walking into his own home, tossing his shoes off, and laying his jacket over the back of a sofa. Then he saw a man walking out of the shadows.

The guy who came down the hall was another police officer. If Widow had to guess, it was the chief. He carried himself with the confidence only a veteran officer had.

The guy had sandpapery red skin and thick white hair that was growing out of a buzz cut. In the military, they would have reminded him it was time for a trim because his hair was touching his ears. The sides and the top were of equal length. Widow made special note of how thick it was because usually in a man his age, there was visible scalp, but this guy's head was covered in white hair. He had high cheekbones and deep-set eyes that seemed almost hidden because of how brown they were and how deep they were on his face.

The guy stopped at the center of the bullpen and looked over at Widow. He held a cup of coffee, or maybe hot tea, in one hand. It was in a medium-sized paper to-go cup, like from a coffee shop. Maybe he had gotten it from the general store. Maybe it had been brewed from the coffee beans Widow had ridden in with.

The guy halted where he was and then said with a deep, crisp voice, "Who are you?"

Widow said, "I'm nobody. Just a guy who was in the wrong place at the wrong time, and now I'm sitting in your jail."

The cop breathed in heavily and walked over to a desk, past the bullpen in the corner, into an office space with no door. Widow couldn't read the name on the door because of the distance, but he guessed this guy was definitely the police chief. Why else would he have his own office space?

The chief set his coffee down on the desk and then took off his heavy, cropped jacket. It had the same symbols on the sleeves as that of the Lakota police badge on Officer Red Cloud's shield. Then the guy walked out of his office, past the bullpen, and over to Widow's cell. He stopped three feet away and looked Widow up and down.

The guy was tall, about five, ten or maybe six feet, and he had a powerful stare—a cop stare plus a strong Native American stare, as if he was a descendant of warriors of the old world. Widow noticed the name on his nameplate that was set just above a pocket on his left breast, and he sighed. He felt he might be in more trouble than he wanted to be in because the nameplate said, "*Red Cloud*."

The guy was Officer Red Cloud's father—Chief Red Cloud.

11

Red Cloud, the father, said, "I asked you who you are."

"Widow."

"Widow? First name or last?"

"Last," Widow said.

"What's your first name, son?"

"Jack."

"Jack, why the hell are you in my jail?"

"I was arrested."

The chief rolled his eyes and then said, "I meant, why are you in there? What did you do? What charge?"

"I was arrested by a female officer. I wasn't told what the charges were. Actually, I haven't even been officially booked or read my rights."

The chief rolled his eyes again and then gave Widow a hard stare, looking him up and down again.

"I guess I'm in here for assaulting a police officer."

The guy said, "That's my daughter. Did you try to hit on her or something?"

But he didn't ask, as if he believed it. He asked, more like it hadn't been the first time his daughter had arrested someone… wrongly.

"Not exactly. She didn't arrest me for that. She wasn't the officer I assaulted." Widow paused a beat and added, "Allegedly assaulted."

A confused look came over Chief Red Cloud's face. He broke his stare with Widow and stepped away to walk over to a random desk that appeared to be empty. He sat down on top of it and pulled a cell phone out of his pocket and stared at it a moment, then dialed a number. Someone must've answered, because he looked up and appeared to be listening.

"Okay. So why's he here in my cell?" he asked.

He listened some more, and then he said, "Amita, you can't just leave him here."

Another pause and another moment of listening to her, and then Chief Red Cloud asked, "What federal agents?"

He paused a beat and then asked, "Where are they from?"

He listened some more and then said, "Amita, they don't have jurisdiction here. They should've cleared any operations with us first. So explain to me why this guy assaulted them and why they aren't here right now filing a grievance."

He listened some more this time, much longer. Widow guessed she was explaining the situation to him. The guy listened for a long time and said nothing.

Widow couldn't really make out the details. What he put together was that these two federal agents weren't supposed to be on the reservation in the first place, and that was all he was interested in. That they weren't supposed to be there meant they were running a secret operation, or they were off the books. Suddenly, Widow felt better about his situation because if they were off the books, they couldn't charge him for anything, and he'd be out of there within forty-eight hours. If they were running a secret operation, they still couldn't hold him without charging him. So either way, he was going to be a free man and back on the road.

The chief said, "Amita. Amita. Stop. Stop. Listen to me. Calm down. Stop looking for those guys and get your ass back here. I don't care about who they work for. They can't operate here without my knowledge. Okay?"

Then he switched the phone off.

Chief Red Cloud looked back up at Widow and walked over to the cell again.

Widow said, "Trouble?"

"It appears you're a lucky young man. My daughter tells me you beat up two guys who were pushing and shoving her?"

Widow nodded.

"For that, I thank you for being a gentleman and trying to help her out, but you still can't go around beating up people. Not on my land. Do you understand me?"

Widow nodded.

"It turns out that these two guys are federal agents, and that's why she arrested you. Now perhaps she overreacted, but she's a good cop. A very good cop. She loves her people, and I think she reacted out of shock and surprise because you sneaked up on them. And maybe you scared her. No offense, but you're a frightening customer."

Widow nodded again. He wasn't offended. He was used to people fearing him.

"Are you going to let me out?"

"Not yet. We have to hold you because you assaulted two officers of the US government." He said it like he harbored no warm, fuzzy feelings toward the federal government. Growing up in America knowing that your government had robbed your people of their lands and systematically murdered most of them to the point of extinction could definitely put a damper on a man's patriotism. But Chief Red Cloud had proven himself to be a reasonable father and a good cop, in Widow's eyes.

Widow asked, "When then?"

"I don't know. Amita and I will discuss it when she comes back. She said she went back to find the agents you put down, and they were gone. One part of the good news is that they must be alive. She said you hit one of them so hard he didn't get back up. But apparently, he's up. The other part of the good news is that they still haven't contacted us. So if we don't hear from them by morning, I'm okay with cutting you loose."

Widow smiled and said, "That works for me. Free room for the night."

"And board. Law says we have to feed you at least two meals a day. You hungry?"

"No, thanks. I have no appetite right now."

The chief nodded.

"I'll take a cup of coffee if you got it, though."

The chief smiled. "I don't have any here. Not made. But I know what to do."

He walked into his office and backed out with his radio. He got on it and called Amita. "Come in, Amita."

"What now? Why not call me back on the phone?" she called back over the air.

"I wanted to make sure you were in your car."

"Well, I am. So what?"

"Stop back at the general store on your way and pick up a medium coffee. Hold on a second," Chief Red Cloud said. He moved his mouth away from the radio and released the talk button. "How do you want your coffee?"

Widow said, "Black." He smiled because he realized that not only was this better than staying in a motel because it was free, but he was also getting room service. And the officer who arrested him was getting it, which gave him a small sense of satisfaction. Incremental revenge could sometimes be the best kind of revenge.

The chief said, "Bring the coffee. Black. No cream. No sugar. Got it?"

Static crackled over the speaker for a second, and then Amita Red Cloud's voice came back over, calm and collected. She said, "Ten-four."

There was no other reply, no snappy comeback, no sign of distaste that her father was treating her prisoner like a guest instead of a dishonest, violent white man. Widow felt an apology from her would do the trick, but he didn't expect to get one and didn't want to push her like her father was doing. He was the chief of police and her father, and he could push her all he wanted and get away with it. But Widow didn't want to be on her bad side any more than he already was.

Chief Red Cloud said, "My daughter's a wonderful person, but she's stubborn and takes her heritage to heart. Not your fault. Don't take it personally. You're a stranger from a different world—an idealistic world. Out there, society pities the Indian. Here, we don't want pity. We're a proud people. You'll find that many residents will feel hostile toward you because you're an outsider and a white man. But not by the law and not in my house and not by my daughter. I want you to know that, from a legal standpoint, what you did was wrong. But you didn't know who those guys were. And that was their fault. They shouldn't be out on the reservation ordering around any of my officers—and especially not my daughter.

"When she gets here, she and I are going to have a talk about this. I'll find out more about what's going on with these two guys. But none of that concerns you. From my perspective, it seems like a misunderstanding that went too far."

Widow nodded and said, "It happens."

He was impressed with Amita's father. Really, he was impressed with both of them, a father-daughter team. Widow thought back to his own mother. If she had still been alive, maybe they would've been a mother and son team. He should've called her sooner instead of waiting until she had been shot to return home.

His mother had been murdered. But that was after he hadn't spoken to her for sixteen years. That was his only regret in life.

If she had been alive, he might still live in Killian Crossing, working for her as one of her deputies. It wasn't the life he had wanted, but at least in that scenario, she'd still be alive.

12

Officer Amita Red Cloud pulled into the lot of the police station and parked behind her father's Chevy Silverado. She killed the engine and stepped out of her police car.

Leaning back into the vehicle, she grabbed her gear and a hot black coffee she hoped was for her father but feared was for their prisoner. She shut the door and stomped her way through the lot to the rear entrance. She unlocked the door and walked in.

As she walked into the station, the sight before her made her freeze in place and stare wide-eyed. Her father sat in a chair, pulled up in front of the prisoner's cell. His cell door was wide open. Her prisoner sat in a wheeled office chair that her father had apparently rolled over to him and allowed him to use. He was halfway out of his cell. The prisoner was sitting and talking with her father, laughing.

She exclaimed, "Dad! What the hell's going on?"

Chief Red Cloud sat upright and then got up to his feet. She watched the smile drain from his face. He looked at her and splayed his hands, trying to let her know he meant no harm. Amita felt her blood boiling. Her father was breaking all kinds of protocols and security measures. Not to mention public safety concerns.

Red Cloud said, "Amita, calm down. Before you get all fired up, just listen to me."

Amita said, "Dad! This man is my prisoner!"

"He is technically detained, but you didn't arrest him or charge him or book him. So he's not a prisoner. He's a detained suspect. And so far, no one has come forward and filed charges against him."

"What the hell do you think I've been out there trying to do? I've searched and searched for those guys. I'm sure they'll want to press charges against him. He beat the shit out of them—and in plain view of me."

Red Cloud breathed in and breathed out slowly, which was a thing Widow imagined fathers often did with their children to communicate with them they needed to watch the line they were crossing.

Amita said, "This guy you're sitting with and chatting it up just beat up two federal agents. There's no question of guilt. I saw him do it. I don't care what his reasons are. And neither will the guys he beat up. These guys were assholes, but I guarantee they'll be back for him."

Red Cloud thought for a moment, and then he said, "Why don't you come over here and join us. Explain it to both of us."

"Both of you?" Amita said. "I don't have to explain anything to him. He's a prisoner!"

"Amita! He is not a prisoner! You failed to charge him, book him, fingerprint him, or read him his rights. We may live on a reservation, but this is still the United States, and we have a little thing called the Constitution to consider. He has a right to face his accusers and a right to due process. So far, there've been no accusers, and you have neglected to give him due process. We can give him due process now. So sit with us and tell us about it. He has a right to know the details. If we charge him with assault on a cop, the first thing his lawyer is going to say is that he has a right to know everything about the situation so that he can stage a proper defense."

Amita stood quietly for a long moment.

Widow stared at her, hoping she didn't catch on to the fact that he was uncontrollably attracted to her. He had no plans of dating or getting attached or getting married or having a house, a dog, or a picket fence. Those things didn't belong in his life. But she made him reconsider.

He looked down at the white tile floor and stayed in his seat. He kept his hands on his lap and in plain view of Amita Red Cloud because his gut told him that if he raised them even a little, she'd shoot him where he sat. There was a lot of hostility aimed his way, and he wasn't really sure why. He guessed it might be the situation he had interrupted—two federal agents pushing her around. She seemed to be a proud Native American—a woman and a cop, to boot.

She'd overcome a lot of adversity, and Widow respected that. Perhaps the problem was that a man had saved her. Or perhaps there was some other reason she was angry. She definitely held a grudge against him.

She said, "Dad…" And then she trailed off and agreed to sit with them. She handed the coffee to Chief Red Cloud, and he walked over and gave it to Widow.

He smiled a good hearty smile and said, "Here. Now the three of us can sit and figure this out. Mr. Widow was just telling me about himself. He has an interesting story. His mother was a sheriff back in Mississippi."

"Was?" Amita asked.

"Unfortunately, she moved on a while ago," Red Cloud said.

Widow nodded and stayed quiet. He noticed that Red Cloud had said "moved on" instead of "passed on," which he had never heard before. He didn't ask, but he wondered if it was a view the Lakota people held about death—like instead of dying, they transcended—because the phrase suggested a person had left rather than died.

Red Cloud said, "Mr. Widow is now a wanderer."

Amita remained standing for a minute, as if making a special point that she was the last to sit, and then she pulled a chair from the bullpen. It didn't have wheels like the one that her father had pulled out, and so it screeched across the floor when she moved it. She set it to Widow's right. Close to her father, but far from Widow's reach.

Amita said, "Interesting. So in your wandering, do you like beating up cops? Saving women in distress?"

"What's your problem with me?" Widow asked without thinking about it. A reaction.

Amita said, "I don't like a stranger coming to my reservation, my home, and beating up on federal agents! I don't like that you just assumed I needed your help! I'm a police officer! You don't rescue me! I rescue you!"

Her eyes reddened, and her face darkened like she was on the verge of exploding. Widow didn't feel anger. He didn't feel regret about asking his question point-blank either. Now he understood her. She'd faced a lot of the obstacles that his own mother must've faced. He didn't blame her for being headstrong. She probably had to be.

Red Cloud said, "Amita! Mr. Widow isn't a criminal! He's our guest until those two agents walk through that door and tell me they want to press charges against him. The Constitution says innocent until proven guilty. Let's act like we believe in that."

Amita stayed quiet and looked away for a moment, trying to compose herself, and then she looked back and faked a smile at Widow.

He knew the expression of someone staring at another person with daggers in their eyes, but he'd never seen a smile with daggers. He said, "It's okay. I don't need special treatment or any kind of apology. I respect Officer Red Cloud. And I respect the law. I really thought that I was helping you out back there. That's why I intervened. I saw those guys pushing you, and I guess my instincts got ahead of my better judgment."

Amita swallowed hard, like she was forcing down her disdain. Then she composed herself and asked, "Why did you think I was in danger? Because I'm a little woman, and they were two big guys?"

Widow shook his head and said, "Not at all. I saw two civilians poking and prodding an officer of the law. That set me off first. Let's just say that besides my mother, I've known a lot of cops." He paused a beat and looked around the room. Then he looked back at Amita and said, "A woman of the law in potential danger sets me off. I know now you could've handled it, but I wasn't sure if you knew those guys were armed. Look, I saw a gun tucked into each of their waistbands, and I reacted. I believe in first reaction."

"What's first reaction?"

"It means react before you have something to react to."

"Like shoot first?"

Widow nodded and stayed quiet.

Red Cloud said, "Act first. Ask for forgiveness and not permission sort of attitude?"

Widow nodded, and then he said, "In some situations, it's best to act first and plan later."

Amita stayed quiet.

Widow said, "I sincerely apologize to you. And if those guys come around again, I'll apologize to them too."

Amita said nothing.

"There you have it. Widow is sorry. Now accept his apology," Red Cloud said.

Amita said, "I'm sorry that maybe I overreacted. And I thank you for your concern. Maybe those guys won't come in to press charges, anyway. Actually, I know they won't, so I guess you're off the hook."

Widow smiled. "Thank you. The apology isn't necessary."

Red Cloud asked, "So what the hell were two agents doing on my reservation, anyway?"

Amita looked at Widow and must've decided he was privy to the information because she said, "They had FBI badges. Said they were here looking for someone."

"Why didn't they come by and tell me first?"

"They came by yesterday. You were out."

"You went off alone with them? Why didn't you radio me?"

"Dad, I'm perfectly capable of liaising with a couple of FBI agents without you."

"You mean you were more interested in impressing them than doing your job properly?"

Amita didn't answer that.

Widow said, "Better to ask for forgiveness over permission."

Amita finally cracked a smile.

"Next time, you call me. So who were these agents looking for?" Red Cloud asked.

Amita stared directly at her father's face, like his reaction was the most important thing ever. Then she said, "Mike Jacobs."

Red Cloud said, "Michael Jacobs? *Your* Mike?"

Amita nodded. Widow assumed that meant she knew the guy they were hunting.

"What does the FBI want with a guy who hasn't been seen here in two years?"

Amita said, "They wouldn't say. They said it was vital that they look around for him. They said they wanted to keep it quiet. That's why I didn't call you. I knew you wouldn't let me help them."

"You're damn right I wouldn't let you! That son of a bitch left you heartbroken two years ago, and he ran off and left his old grandpa to live way out there alone. Jacobs has no respect for his elders." Red Cloud said and pointed out in the distance to the north.

Widow stirred for the first time throughout this conversation, shifted in his seat.

Both Red Clouds looked at him.

"What? You think that this is all about my ex-boyfriend?" Amita asked.

Widow shook his head and said, "No. But I wouldn't expect that a couple of agents would be here searching for your ex-boyfriend, and you just happened to be the cop who answered the door when they came through."

"Well, that's what happened. So what is it you're thinking? Something's bothering you. It's written all over your face."

Widow said, "What's bothering me is that something's not right with these FBI agents."

Red Cloud said, "What do you mean?"

Widow looked at him and then back at Amita, and he said, "FBI agents don't behave like that. FBI agents call ahead and check in with local law enforcement. The FBI has strict protocols in place for dealing with local cops, and then there are issues of jurisdiction. And FBI agents don't dress like those guys—they were rugged and wore street clothes. FBI guys normally wear suits."

Both Red Clouds looked at each other and then back at Widow.

Red Cloud said, "Undercover cops dress rugged all the time."

Widow nodded and said, "Maybe. But those guys were ex-military. Had to be. Trust me, I know."

"So what?" Amita said.

Widow said, "Cops dress rugged, sure. And a lot of ex-military become cops when they get out of uniform. They trade one uniform for the other."

The Red Clouds nodded.

"But have you ever looked up how to apply to be a special agent with the FBI?" Widow asked.

Amita nodded and said, "I've always wanted to be a special agent. What about it?"

"Then, you know how rigorous the application process is and all the stipulations they have to get in?"

Amita nodded.

Widow said, "The most common way to get in is to get a law degree."

She nodded again.

Widow said, "How many guys do you know who went into the military, got a law degree, and then joined the FBI?"

The Red Clouds stared at him and didn't answer.

"It's possible. There's the JAG Corps, but the military requires that they serve a while after graduating. The odds of both guys having gone that route aren't high," Widow said.

"Maybe they served four years and then went to law school after," Amita said.

"It's possible, but I don't think so. These guys were military lifers. It was in their stances and the way they dressed. Everything about them said military."

Red Cloud asked, "What're you saying?"

"These guys aren't FBI. No way."

13

At that moment, a silence fell over the station house. It was broken after a minute by the whir of a heater kicking on and the vents above exhaling warm air. Thin ribbons of thread hung from the scattered vents and whipped around from the sudden rush of air.

Widow gazed up at the ceiling on some natural impulse and then back down at Amita Red Cloud, who was thumbing her lip as if trying to keep herself from chewing on her nails. She inserted the thumb and then withdrew it. Inserted it again, and then withdrew it.

Finally, Chief Red Cloud asked, "So what agency are they?"

Widow stayed quiet.

Red Cloud looked at his daughter and asked, "Did you see their badges?"

Amita nodded, and then she said, "They had FBI badges. No doubt about it. I inspected the seal myself, but…" She trailed off and didn't continue her sentence.

Red Cloud asked, "But what?"

"Widow's right. They weren't FBI," Amita said.

"You saw their badges. What do you mean they weren't FBI?"

"Their badges were real."

"So how were they not FBI?"

Amita paused a beat, and then she said, "He's right. There was something off about them. They had real badges. And they certainly acted like feds. But they weren't right. Something about them didn't fit."

"So why did you agree to take these guys out on the reservation? And alone? Why didn't you radio me?"

"I'm sorry, Dad. I know I should've radioed you. It was a mistake. I just thought… I just thought—"

"You just thought you could impress them," he interrupted, "and you were distracted about Michael Jacobs."

Amita said, "I'm sorry. Yes. I was so excited the FBI was here. I thought they were real. I didn't think about protocols. I didn't think to confirm their identities with the office. And they told me there was no time. They said they had just chased the guy onto the reservation."

"That was stupid of you, Amita. You were distracted, and you let these two strangers into our community. They could've hurt you. Widow did the right thing."

Amita looked at Widow.

He stayed quiet.

She said, "They said it was urgent. I'm sorry, Dad."

Widow said, "They were lying."

"How the hell would you know?" she asked.

"The FBI doesn't have a field office in Wyoming."

Amita asked, "So what?"

"The closest one is in Salt Lake City. Which I was just in yesterday."

"So?"

"Salt Lake City is a long way from here."

"Which means?"

"Which means these guys had plenty of time to tell you they were in the area. Two FBI agents drive all the way from Salt Lake City? I buy that. But two guys claiming to be FBI and just showing up out of the blue without calling ahead and confirming with local law enforcement that they were coming through? That's harder to swallow. Their office could've easily called ahead while they were on the road—plenty of time with that distance. They wouldn't just pop up unannounced unless they had something to hide.

"Also, FBI badges are available on the internet. Anyone can get a fake badge that looks pretty real online."

Red Cloud said, "So if they weren't FBI, who were they? And if they aren't federal agents, we need to find them and arrest them. Posing as a federal agent is illegal."

Widow said, "I didn't say they weren't federal agents. They were definitely agents."

"Well, if they aren't FBI, who do they work for?" Amita asked.

Widow said, "That's a good question."

Red Cloud said, "We should find out. We'll call the FBI office in the morning."

Widow stayed quiet.

Amita looked at Widow. "And what about him?"

Red Cloud said, "Mr. Widow, as of now, you are free. We apologize for the misunderstanding."

Red Cloud looked at his watch, and then he said, "It's late. I'm afraid you missed the shuttle to Tower Junction. Do you have a place to stay for the night?"

Widow shook his head.

"You can stay here. You were going to have to stay the night in a cell, anyway. We can leave the doors open for you. Just don't leave until the morning. The temperatures are going to drop into the low teens tonight. We don't want you out there freezing to death."

Amita smiled for the first time, and Widow noted it. He felt like she was smiling at the thought of him freezing to death.

Amita said, "I can drive him. There's no reason to hold him up if we're going to let him go."

Red Cloud said, "No. He'd better stay the night. In the morning, you can take him, and then you can coordinate with the police in Tower Junction and check the hospital there for any sign of these guys. Maybe they checked themselves in."

A blank expression fell over her face. It meant nothing to Widow, but he saw her father recognized it. It must've meant she was disappointed. Widow let go of his contempt for Amita's actions. He wasn't the kind of guy to hold a grudge. Life was too short for grudges.

They talked a little more, but said nothing else about the two guys. After a while, Chief Red Cloud called it a night. They both said their good-nights to Widow and left him alone. The station house lights were dimmed to a tolerable shade so Widow could sleep.

He returned the chairs to their original places and walked back into his cell. The station house was plenty warm, so Widow pulled off the gray fleece and then the shirt and folded them neatly and tucked them underneath the cot on the floor. Then he sat on the bed. The springs bounced and squeaked under his weight, but they weren't uncomfortable.

Widow smiled because he thought it was funny that he was back in a jail cell, and it was his own choice.

14

THE DAYLIGHT SEEPED in through several thick casement windows with crisscrossed layers of metal minibars embedded in the glass. Widow woke up bright and early—6:15 a.m., according to the clock on the far wall. But it wasn't his body clock that had awoken him so early. It was the rustling noises of Amita Red Cloud as she entered the station house.

She came in, carrying a to-go cup with coffee in it from the general store again.

Widow sat upright and smiled. He thought maybe Amita had gone home and about the talk they had the night before. He imagined that she and her father had gone outside and talked more in the parking lot. Chief Red Cloud probably calmed his daughter down. Maybe now she was feeling warmer toward Widow. So on her way to the jail, she had stopped and grabbed him a cup of coffee—a peace offering.

Then he realized he had been mistaken about her warming up to him because she took a sip of the coffee and placed it on a desk. She had bought one for herself and nothing for him.

She walked over to his cell and forced a smile. Then she asked, "Ready?"

Widow stood up and stretched.

She stared. Amita saw he had caught her gazing at him, but it didn't stop her from looking. She traced the tattoos that covered his body, and then she saw old scars underneath some of them. There was nothing major on his front side. She continued to gloss him over and then made eye contact. She asked, "Where are your clothes?"

Widow turned, bent down, and picked them up and showed them to her. When he turned, she had gotten a glance at his back and the three-circle scars in a triangle on the top middle of it. They looked like craters, that had been dug out. Bullet wounds from a past long ago.

He stayed quiet as he shuffled his fingers through his shirt, straightened out the sleeves, and slipped the shirt on. Next, he picked up the fleece and slipped it on.

"What the hell happened to your back?"

"It's nothing."

"Gunshot wounds?"

Widow nodded.

"So, you wanna tell me about that?"

"Nothing to tell."

Amita stared at him, unwilling to let it go.

Widow said, "I was in the military. I was a cop. Got shot in the back once. Really nothing else to say about it."

Amita stepped back and said, "Let's go."

Widow asked, "Where to?"

"You're leaving the reservation."

"Why? Did you find the guys?"

"No. You aren't going to court or anything like that. Like my dad said, you're a free man, but I want you off the reservation. So I'm taking you to Tower Junction."

Widow paused a beat, and then he said, "So I'm not under arrest or detainment any longer?"

Amita nodded.

He asked, "So why do I have to leave? Maybe I want to stay."

Amita froze in front of him. She asked, "Do you want to stay?"

Widow shook his head and said, "Not particularly. I just don't like being told where I can't be."

"Well, you *can't* stay on Red Rain Reservation," she said. "Look, it's best for all. Right now, we have no reason to hold you. There's nothing here to see. You should leave before it's too late."

He stayed quiet.

Amita handed him his passport and asked, "You still got the rest of your stuff?"

He nodded.

Amita pointed toward the door again and cleared her throat like it was a command. Like, *Move on, prisoner.*

They reached the door, and Widow opened it. He walked out, and she followed and closed it behind her. Widow noticed she had left her coffee and thought it would be cold by the time she came back to it, but he said nothing about it. Why should he?

The cold hit him like a gale force, the kind that came from winters in Wyoming. Cold he had expected, but this was extreme. He didn't know what the temperature was, but it was low. The ground outside was moist, like the sunrise had melted some of the snow, but not all of it. Not by a long shot.

Widow didn't even remember hearing it snow the night before, but then again, he wasn't used to snow. He guessed that most snow fell silently.

As he approached the only police cruiser in the lot, he turned and looked up at the sky. It was hazy, but sunlight stabbed through, making holes in the gloom.

Widow walked to the passenger door of the police car and waited. Amita stopped at the driver's side and looked up at him over the top of the car, past the light bar. She said, "Nope. No way. You sit in the back."

Widow shrugged but didn't argue. He was done trying to figure her out. And he realized it was best for him to leave. What if those guys returned and wanted payback? This way, he didn't have to endure that or jail time or any more of Amita Red Cloud's wonderful hospitality. He opened the door, dumped himself down on the rear bench, and slammed the door shut. At least this time, he wasn't in handcuffs. That thought gave him some relief.

Amita got in after him and she fired up the cruiser. The engine hummed low. Widow felt the blast from the air vents as the heater struggled to heat the interior of the car. Amita slipped the gear into reverse, backed up, and pulled away from the lot.

They drove onto the main road. She drove slowly over the thick snow. The white powder kicked up under the tires. It felt like they were driving on sand.

They drove past the signs to the reservation and back onto Grand Loop Road.

Suddenly, Amita said, "I didn't search you because I didn't want to be within your reach. That's why I left the cuffs on you until you were in the cage."

"What?"

"Last night. In case you wondered why I didn't search you."

Widow nodded, said, "I wasn't even thinking about it."

Except he was. He thought, *I could've had a gun.*

But he hadn't, and nothing had happened anyway. As of now, he was getting off after having beaten up two federal agents from some agency he still hadn't figured out yet. He ignored her and turned his head and stared out the window.

He thought, *None of my business.*

The rest of the drive was silent until Amita turned on the radio. The channel was tuned to a morning show from somewhere else in the county. Static buzzed and the voice went in and out. The guy on the radio gave the weather report and said that a hard blizzard they were tracking had moved to the north last night and had been on a trajectory to head away from the territory—originally. But it had made a dramatic turnaround and was now headed straight for the reservation and Tower Junction. The radio predicted it would be a full-blown blizzard by nightfall.

Amita shook her head at the radio and said, "See. You should leave anyway. You don't want to be stuck here when that thing hits us. Snowstorms here are no joke. You don't even have the right clothes. Storms kill tourists all the time because they come up here and venture into the mountains and don't plan for them."

She didn't know what kinds of weather he had been in. Widow had been in a snowstorm before. He had been stationed briefly in Antarctica once, as well as stuck undercover on a mountain range in South Asia during a polar vortex.

Widow looked at her eyes in the rearview mirror as she spoke. He started to speak, but then he thought better of it. There was no point in being nice to her now. He stayed quiet.

15

GRAND LOOP ROAD wasn't nearly as snowed over as the reservation had been, probably because there was an adequate amount of traffic plowing tracks through the snow. The long, winding stretch of road had diverse scenery. That was for damn sure. One second, Widow was looking out the window at snow-covered rock formations, and the next, he saw snow-covered plains and trees. At one point, he'd seen a snow-covered caribou or deer or moose. He wasn't certain what kind of animal it was. It was something big with large treelike antlers. The creature stopped at a nearby stream that was half frozen, and it dipped its head down to take a drink.

Widow looked forward and saw the road wind some more, and finally, they came up on the outskirts of a settlement that must've been Tower Junction. The first buildings in sight were residential houses and various small subdivisions. There was a service drive that turned off and paralleled the road and then jutted north. On the corner, he saw a gas station. Amita turned off the road and headed toward it. She looped around and pulled into the bay and parked the car.

She said, "Mr. Widow, this is your stop."

Widow opened the door to get out, but he stopped. He looked forward at her and said, "I'm not a bad guy. I was only trying to help you. Part of me wishes we could start over, but I guess it doesn't matter now. But for what it's worth, I don't think you're a bad cop. Everyone makes mistakes."

Amita Red Cloud turned and looked back at him. She breathed a heavy sigh, and then she asked, "Are you hungry?"

Widow said, "I could eat. I can always eat."

She said, "There's a diner around the corner. Sometimes I'll drive here and go there just to get away. You like to join me for breakfast?"

Widow nodded.

Amita turned to face the nose of the car and shifted back to drive. Widow sat back, and they drove back out of the gas station lot and turned onto another snow-covered road that paralleled a chain-link fence. Widow could barely see the dotted yellow line in the center of the road. Then the weather turned on them. Snow began trickling out of the sky. Clouds hung overhead, shading the town and the roads.

Widow looked at a street sign and took note that this was now Main Street.

They drove only a couple of blocks. Amita pulled the car into the parking lot of a restaurant called *Terry's Diner*.

She got out, and Widow got out the rear door. He immediately noticed the thick, muddy snow on the ground, and he stepped cautiously. He wondered if he needed snowshoes.

Amita walked around the front of the car and looked at him standing there, peering down at his feet like a big dumb ape, which was pretty much what she thought of him. Then she couldn't help but smile.

Widow asked, "What's so funny?"

"Nothing. Just wondering if you ever saw snow before?"

Widow nodded, said, "It's been a while."

"There was snow yesterday at the res. You walked through it all afternoon."

"It didn't snow. Just had snow already on the ground. And it wasn't like this, not nearly as thick and high."

Amita said, "Come on. Let's get inside. Unless you want to stand there all day and wait till the snow comes down, turns you into a snowman?"

"Inside sounds good. It's cold."

"All you've got on is a fleece. And this is nothing. Tonight, it's going to be freezing, especially dangerous if that snowstorm passes over us."

He nodded.

"I can't stay long. Just breakfast. Then I have to head back and help buckle everything down for the night."

Widow stayed quiet.

They entered through a single push-and-pull glass door with a bell way up on the top corner. It dinged as they entered. The doorframe was strangely thin. It reminded him of the doorways on a submarine. He instinctively ducked his head down like he was entering the command deck.

Inside, the diner was plain. Plain walls. Plain long service counter. Plain booths along the walls and windows. Nothing special about it.

Widow liked these kinds of diners. They were a part of the American landscape. He preferred them over the traditional chain brands. He liked the concealment and the bareness of places that he had heard some people describe as "holes in the wall." Plus, there was a good feeling he got knowing he was supporting a local business and not a big chain restaurant. So far, Widow had been all over the southwestern United States, and he had stopped for coffee at a host of places—diners, IHOPs, Waffle House, coffee shops, bars, restaurants, and Starbucks. He liked coffee because it was like fuel for his body. He walked a lot, and he stopped for coffee.

Not all coffee was created equal. He had found that, often, the local establishment had the best coffee. They kept it fresher. There was a Starbucks in San Diego, where he had stopped one day. He had ordered the coffee of the day. It was called Pumpkin Spice. It was pretty good. Good enough for him to remember it and record it in his worthwhile memory files.

Amita didn't ask where Widow wanted to sit. She simply walked all the way to the back corner booth. It had an excellent view of the road and the door. She sat down on the west side, which left Widow with only two options—sit next to her on the same bench or sit across from her. Of course, the obvious choice was to sit across from her. That was what he was sure she had intended. The only problem with this was that it left his back to the front door. And Widow didn't like that. He didn't like having a blindside. Especially not his back. This was understandable because he had been shot in the back before, and she knew that. She had seen the results.

Another thought running through his head was that even though he respected Amita Red Cloud, he didn't trust her. What if this was all a ploy to get him into another jurisdiction, and once she got him sitting down and fed and full, then the two agents from whatever agency would enter from behind him and get the drop on him? Not a plausible scenario, not likely, but he had the thought just the same.

Amita looked up at him and asked, "You gonna sit?"

Widow plopped himself down on the bench across from her and smiled.

He reached over and grabbed a menu, which had already been placed on the table. He opened it up and asked, "So, what's good here?"

Amita smiled at him and said, "Nothing." Then she laughed for the first time since he had met her.

Startled by it, he jerked his head up at her like she had thrown water in his face. He quickly regained composure and laughed with her.

"Seriously, the food here isn't the best, but it's the closest place. And you get used to it."

"They got good coffee?"

"Coffee isn't bad," she said, and then she paused and said, "Shit!"

"What?"

"I left my coffee back at the station. That was three bucks at the general store. It's pretty good coffee."

Widow smiled.

"Guess I can reheat it later."

Amita grabbed her menu and glanced over it. The glossy cover reflected the lights from above and glimmered into Widow's eyes. It reminded him of a sniper scope from off in the distance when the sunlight beams down and gives away an enemy's position.

The waitress walked over. Her name tag said she was Maggie. Maggie was possibly Amita's age, which Widow guessed was somewhere around twenty-five. She had straight auburn hair and a nose with a tiny cluster of freckles, like a constellation of stars. She smelled of perfume with a good dose of cigarette smoke underneath, like she had just returned from a smoke break and had sprayed herself to cover the smell. The waitress was medium height and had an average build, but Widow noticed she had long fingers. They were abnormally long for a person of her size.

She smiled a big, friendly smile and said, "Officer Amita, how are you doing today?"

Amita nodded, but didn't answer the question. And Maggie didn't wait. She turned to Widow with a look of great interest on her face. She said, "Now, honey, you've found yourself a boyfriend? My, oh my."

Widow smiled. He hadn't seen that coming.

Amita shook her head vigorously. Widow took special note of it but didn't let it hurt his feelings. Instead, he said, "She had me in handcuffs last night."

Which was technically true.

Maggie smiled and turned a shade of red. Amita turned crimson and then a deep shade of purple and stared at Widow with deadly eyes.

Widow quickly retracted his statement with, "Only kidding. Officer Red Cloud arrested me last night over a misunderstanding. Now we're friends. That's all."

Maggie shot him a look of confusion, but didn't question his statement.

Amita said, "That's all. Let's order."

"What should I get?"

Maggie listed the specials, but Amita waved her hand and said, "Texas BLT sandwiches and eggs for both of us. Scrambled. And coffee."

"And toast," Widow said.

Maggie smiled at him and took their menus. She walked away and returned shortly after with silverware. Then she left again and returned five minutes later with two empty coffee mugs and a dark-blue carafe of fresh, hot coffee. She placed the mugs down in front of them and poured each a cup of coffee.

After Maggie was gone, Amita said, "Hey, the handcuff thing isn't funny. I've got to live with these people."

"She thought it was funny."

"Look, I'm buying you breakfast, okay, because my dad asked me to. And I feel a little bad about last night. I really am a good cop."

"I know you are. A little overzealous, maybe, but lots of great cops have been. Better to be overly cautious than lazy and ignorant. I've seen both."

"Thanks," she said, but wasn't sure if he was complimenting her or not.

Silence fell between them for a moment, and Widow took a sip of his coffee. It was hot and good. Not the best, not as good as the Pumpkin Spice from the Starbucks in San Diego, but it was far from the worst. He looked up and watched Amita pour an avalanche of sugar into hers. It must have been five or six spoonfuls. Then she picked up a Splenda and tore it open and drizzled it into the coffee.

No wonder you're so high-strung, he thought and then said, "Tell me about Mike Jacobs."

She looked up at him. A strange look in her eyes. Sadness? Regret? Widow wasn't sure, but there was a lot of pain there.

"Mike was my high school sweetheart. He always wanted to leave the reservation. Leave his grandfather to live alone way up near the mountains."

"And you wanted to stay?"

"No. I actually wanted to join the FBI or the DEA or the ATF, any of those agencies. I wanted to travel and get out of here too. But my dad always said that my life was here. It's important to him I stick around and help him police the people."

"You two are alone?"

"There's a desk lady who runs the telephones four days a week, and then there are three other guys that come on in the warmer months. Henry Little is deputized. But in the winter, many people head south or keep to themselves. It gets freezing, especially in January."

Widow nodded and stayed quiet. He thought about his mother and his grandfather. His grandfather had died before he was born. His mother had stayed and taken over his grandfather's role as sheriff—a similar story.

"Mike Jacobs was my boyfriend. We were going to get married a year or two after we graduated from college. But one day, he vanished, gone without a trace. No note. No letter. No phone call. Nothing."

Silence fell between them, and Maggie brought the food out. She said, "Enjoy."

Widow said, "So now these guys are looking for him?"

Amita said, "Yep. Now I think you understand my 'overzealousness,' as you called it. This guy left me and his people years ago, and now he's wanted by some federal agents who are lying about which agency they work for. If they even are feds. Maybe they're hired mercs or something. With Mike, there's no telling what he's gotten himself into."

Widow heard the bell ding behind him, and the door opened and shut. Amita looked up. She stared for a hard second, and then she dismissed it. Widow didn't bother looking.

He surmised from the heavy footsteps that it was a big man —large build. Calm walk. Calm demeanor. Like an old gunfighter. The guy sat down in the booth directly behind Widow. The bench trembled under his weight, and Widow felt it.

Maggie came over to the guy behind Widow and asked what she could get him.

Widow heard a husky voice say, "Coffee." And that was all.

16

AMITA FINISHED her breakfast and slid her plate to the edge of the table. She stacked her silverware on top and wiped her hands on a napkin. Out the window, Widow could see cars and trucks passing slowly down Main Street. Drivers used caution on the snow and followed the tracks that had already been made by previous cars. The street sounds of tires over snow and pavement swept into the diner as new customers opened the door. Widow turned his head and peered at them. It was an older couple. Holding hands and laughing.

Amita smiled.

Widow asked, "So, where does the name Amita come from?"

"It was my great-great-grandmother's name. She was adopted by white parents. Way back. And they named her Amita."

Widow nodded and asked, "Why don't you have a husband or boyfriend now?"

A look traversed her face that said to Widow he might have been crossing a personal boundary. Then again, he didn't really care, since she had arrested him and forced him to spend the night in a cell.

The look vanished, and she shrugged and said, "I have no time for one. Plus, there aren't a lot of suitable candidates on the reservation. Most of the population is old or women. Men grow up and leave."

"Like Jacobs?"

"Like that."

"Sorry. I wouldn't have left if I was your man," he said, but then he thought, *Probably*.

She looked up at him with big brown eyes. She nodded and stayed quiet. It was still a sore subject for her.

Maggie came back to the table, picked up the dishes, and left the check. Widow grabbed it, but Amita got it first and told him she was going to cover it. She pulled out her wallet and left the money on the table. She stood up, put her coat on, and zipped it up over her chest.

She said, "Widow, it was a pleasure. I'm sorry for the hostility. This is no longer your concern. I wish you luck."

She walked away and left Widow to enjoy the rest of his coffee.

Widow watched her go. She walked toward her police cruiser, stopped for an old faded blue Ford pickup to pass through the lot, and nodded a hello at the driver. She continued to her car, opened it, got in, and fired up the engine. Exhaust pooled behind the rear tailpipe. She backed out of her space and pulled away from the lot, and was gone from sight.

17

THE AIR WAFTED in again as new customers entered the diner. It chilled two old guys who sat at the counter. Widow watched as they visibly shivered. He drained his coffee cup and planned out the rest of his day. First, he pulled up what he could remember of the road map in his head and thought about the best way to get out of Yellowstone and move on with his life. Next, he decided he would head south on Grand Loop Road and around Yellowstone Lake. Eventually, he would get to Cheyenne.

Widow stood up and headed out of the restaurant when the guy in the booth behind him said, "Widow?"

Widow turned and looked at the guy, who remained seated. He wore cowboy boots under black chinos and a matching blazer. A thick black sweater was underneath the coat. He had a shoulder rig that poked out when he stretched his hand out to motion for Widow to have a seat.

The guy's face had a ghastly white scar that cut diagonally down the side of his face and took off half of his lower nose. It was hard to look past it. But once he did, Widow saw he had one grayed-out eye and one piercing blue eye. The guy smiled and tried to look as friendly as he could, but given his traits, it wasn't easy.

Widow didn't make any acknowledgment of the guy's scar. He asked, "Do I know you?"

The guy said, "You don't. Please sit down. I'll buy you another coffee."

"How do you know my name?"

"Sit down. Join me."

Widow thought for a moment and shrugged. He dumped himself down in the booth and waited for the guy to explain.

Maggie came over and asked Widow if he wanted another cup of coffee. Widow nodded, and a moment later, she returned with a fresh cup. Black. No carafe this time. Just the coffee.

"So, what can I do for you? How do you know my name?"

"My name is Alex Shepard. I know your name because the two guys you beat up last night at the reservation work for me. I got your name from the database. Red Cloud entered it, but she saw nothing. Not like what I saw."

"What did you see?" Widow asked and realized that maybe he should've kept walking out the door. But then he thought it might not have made a difference. If this guy was implying he had seen Widow's real files, that meant he was part of a shadow agency, like the NSA. Which meant he wouldn't have had much of a chance trying to run. Those two agents were most likely waiting outside in the parking lot, probably in a van or an SUV with tinted windows. And they were probably armed with stun guns.

"I know you aren't just any run-of-the-mill ex-vet turned drifter."

Widow said, "I didn't mean to attack federal agents. I can explain that."

"It was a misunderstanding. I know. I got that from their side of things."

Widow stayed quiet.

"They overstepped their boundaries, and things got out of hand. You were only trying to help Officer Red Cloud. I see that."

"They were harassing her. That's what it looked like to me."

Widow kept Shepard's hands in his peripherals and calculated that if the guy went for his gun, he could beat him down with two moves. One, hot coffee in the face like a smoldering grenade. Two, smash the cup into the guy's good eye. Job done. Case closed.

Shepard nodded and said, "I know. They admitted to me they had stepped out of line. Don't worry. I've put them aside for now. They're waiting back at our motel."

He watched as Widow glanced around the parking lot through the window.

"We're alone. I promise."

"They told the cops at Red Rain they were FBI."

Shepard nodded.

"They aren't FBI. And neither are you."

"No, we're not. We're federal agents."

"I believe that. So who do you work for?"

"We work for the CIA."

"Bullshit! The CIA can't operate on American soil. That's illegal. Big time."

Shepard smiled. The hole where half of his nose used to be turned into one half of an upside-down heart. Widow wondered what had caused such a vicious wound. The guy must've seen some serious wartime.

"I'm telling you the truth."

"If you said the NSA, I might believe you. But the CIA can't operate on American soil. They're bound to spy only on foreign soil. And besides that, the CIA isn't a law enforcement agency."

"Technically, you're both right and wrong," he said, and paused. Then he said, "I've got to tell you that when I learned who you were and that you were the guy who beat up my two agents, I was flummoxed."

Widow furrowed his brow.

"The CIA isn't allowed to operate on American soil. That part's true. But there is one exception." Shepard paused a beat, and then he said, "Indian reservations. We can engage in missions on Indian reservations. There are real-life terrorist cells that are born on Indian reservations. It has always been a genuine concern that one of these groups might rise and try to overthrow the government or create an act of terror for their cause."

Widow stayed quiet. He wasn't really buying it.

"Many Indian people feel a little bitter that we ran them off their lands. They feel oppressed by this. So there is a real concern about them."

Widow asked, "Is that true about the reservations? I never heard that."

"It's true."

"So your two guys were posing as FBI agents to find this Mike Jacobs?"

"That's right."

"What do you know about me?"

Alex Shepard paused a beat, and then he said, "I know you're a Navy SEAL. Used to be. I know that really isn't true, though, is it?"

Widow stared at him.

"Really, you worked for the NCIS. A part of Unit Ten. You worked undercover among the SEALs. Investigating crimes sometimes committed by SEALs. I know you lived a double life. Look at me."

Widow's stare didn't budge.

"I know about living a double life. I've been a spook for decades."

Widow stayed still.

Shepard asked, "What, you don't believe me? I'm a patriot, son. I work for the Agency. Believe me. How do you think I got this scar?"

Shepard leaned in and twisted to the side, giving Widow a close-up of his scar.

"I got struck clear across the face by shrapnel in a bomb blast in Iraq. The blast erupted, blew a soldier to bits, and shards of bone and metal whipped all around the place. I got hit. It took a piece of my nose and left me with one good eye."

Widow said, "It's a cruel world."

"You got that right."

Widow asked, "What do you want from me?"

"I want to make a deal with you."

"I'm listening."

"You help me out, and I'll forget about the assault on my guys."

"You aren't gonna do anything about that anyway. Why don't I just walk now?"

Shepard said, "You're right. I'm not."

"Then I'll just be on my way."

"That's fine. I'm sure Amita will live with your decision," Shepard said.

"What about Amita?"

Maggie came back over to their table and asked if they needed anything else. Widow told her he wanted another cup of coffee. Shepard looked out the window and said nothing.

After she returned with a fresh cup and left again, Shepard looked back at Widow.

He said, "First, I need to clarify that this is a matter of national security. Remember signing a ton of paperwork back when you were in the NCIS? For your security clearance?"

Widow nodded. He remembered it. There were a bunch of lawyers in a small room. He was being inserted into a program that had never existed before, but for a small, elite unit, they sure had plenty of lawyers.

"That means you're still bound to it. Just because you quit the Navy doesn't mean you're out of their control. You can't tell anyone. I'm trusting you with privileged information. Got it?"

Widow said, "Spit it out already."

"I need you to say it."

"I got it."

"Good. That means that even though you don't have top-security clearance, you can still be prosecuted for giving away this information."

"So can you. For telling me," Widow said.

"You got it. That's right."

Widow took a long pull from his coffee and waited.

Shepard said, "Mike Jacobs is one of my guys—a CIA agent. He's my protégé, actually. I handpicked him over a year ago. We have operations in North America. Mostly in Mexico, and sometimes in Canada."

Widow stayed quiet, just listened.

Shepard said, "Two weeks ago, we got intel that there's a terrorist threat here on Red Rain Reservation."

"What intel?" Widow asked.

"That's need to know. Just listen. There's a cell that moves throughout the Lakota world. We've known about them for some time, but mostly just whispers and rumors. No real credible threat. But two weeks ago, we became more interested because we learned that the terrorist cell might have acquired a weapon."

"What kind of weapon?"

"We don't know. We think it's something biological. It's small, something that was being transported in a metal suitcase."

Widow said, "That could be anything."

Shepard nodded, and then he said, "Because Jacobs was from the Red Rain Reservation, he was the obvious candidate to go undercover."

"So, what happened?"

"I sent him in three days ago. I lost contact with him forty-eight hours ago."

Widow stared. The reason those two agents were so pushy clicked in his head. They were trying to find this weapon. He asked, "And then you sent in your two guys?"

"Right. They went in as FBI agents and were told to keep a low profile in case he was in deep cover. Only they ran into you."

Widow looked down at his coffee, felt bad. He said, "Sorry about that."

Shepard shook his head. "Under the circumstances, it's all water under the bridge. Don't worry about it. The crucial thing here is to find Jacobs and the weapon before it's too late."

"What do you want from me? I'm a stranger there. I've only been there one night."

"Look out the window."

Widow craned his neck to look outside.

"Look at the sky," Shepard said and raised his hand and pointed to the horizon to the north.

Widow saw the gray, gloomy clouds that puffed up high above the mountain peaks in the distance. They looked foreboding and menacing and unstoppable, kind of like slow-moving lava where all you could do to escape was to run.

"In the next six hours, the Red Rain Reservation and Tower Junction and all the wilderness and mountains and rivers in between are going to be buried in that snowstorm. The Indians don't trust my guys. They don't trust outsiders. But you've already won over their cops. And that girl, she likes you. I could see that."

Widow doubted that Amita had given any sign that she liked him. He asked, "So what? You want me to go back and ask her to find your missing agent? You could've done that when she was here."

"Widow, that storm is the only thing protecting Red Rain Reservation."

"What does that mean?"

"The reason we think the terrorists have a biological agent is because we don't think it. We know it. That briefcase has a canister inside that contains a weaponized version of the Ebola virus."

Widow stayed quiet.

"Do you know what that sickness can do? We have no cure."

Widow remained silent.

Shepard said, "If Jacobs doesn't surface by the time this storm passes over with news of where the Ebola agent is, then we have no choice but initiate other methods of containment."

"Containment?" Widow asked.

Shepard leaned in close again and said, "I've been ordered to send in a military strike against the reservation."

"Bullshit! The military wouldn't bomb an American target. Not only that, but no pilot would do that either."

"It will not be done by a pilot. We'd use a UCAV."

An unmanned combat aerial vehicle was what he was referring to. Widow looked down at the table. He studied Shepard. He couldn't tell if Shepard was bluffing or not. The whole thing sounded like it was straight out of a spy movie. Then again, that was the thing the CIA did.

Widow had met spooks before. In his experience, he always found it hard to trust them. Saying that they were all on the same team wasn't an accurate description of CIA agents. It was better to say that the agencies in the US were part of the same family. And as with all families, if you dug deep enough, you found members that weren't quite on the same level as the rest of the family.

"Right. So now you see my concern. I don't want to bomb a bunch of helpless people. But it's better to say that the UCAV malfunctioned than to say that the US government brought canisters of Ebola onto American soil and had one stolen by a small terrorist cell. See my point?"

Widow looked out of the window again at the looming snowstorm, and then he looked back at Shepard. He understood. It seemed plausible. If it were true, and this weapon got into the wrong hands, then steps would be taken. The government wasn't in the habit of bombing its own citizens, but then again, the CIA was different. Widow had seen enough in his sixteen years undercover to know that anything was possible.

"So, will you help me find Jacobs and stop a terrorist from releasing a deadly virus?"

"What choice do I have? I'll help. What do I need to know about Jacobs?"

18

SHEPARD GAVE Widow a satellite phone that should work during the calmer phases of the snowstorm. There wasn't much more information he could give him. He didn't know any names or the location of the terrorist cell on Red Rain Reservation.

Widow was going in blind, which was something he was used to.

"I can't tell you how much we appreciate this," Shepard said.

About fifteen minutes after he and Widow had walked out of the diner, they headed back up the winding road to the reservation. They drove in Shepard's gray Ford King Ranch truck. Widow had seen nice trucks before, but this was really something. It was fully loaded with dual captain's chairs in the front cabin. It was the most comfortable ride Widow had in a long time.

He gazed out of the window, mostly because he didn't want to get caught staring at Shepard's scar.

Snow blew in a slow arch across the road, creating a dreary gloom. It wasn't a whiteout but certainly the beginning of one. Widow could see old power lines, but only the stumpy treelike bottoms. The tops vanished in the gray. They looked like the long, bony legs of some unseen creature high above him.

The truck drove steadily over the snowy terrain with no problems. They took it slow because the traffic in front of them was slow. Shepard sped up every chance he got. He'd slow down behind a slow-moving vehicle, and then he'd pass around and speed up again. The King Ranch had an enormous advantage over most of the vehicles because it sat up high, and Shepard could see much farther ahead than the cars they'd passed.

Shepard turned the wheel and moved around a small yellow Beetle that had whining sounds coming from the engine, like it was desperate to survive the terrain. The petite car was buried to the tire rims in the snow.

Shepard swerved around another car. The driver blared his horn.

Widow asked, "Why not alert the real FBI?"

"I wish I could, but we can't let it be known we're responsible for the virus."

Widow nodded. It made sense. The CIA had let some homegrown terrorist cell get their hands on the virus, and now they need to recover it, all the while keeping the whole thing a secret.

"The government is okay with bombing and killing a bunch of innocent people over letting out an embarrassing secret?" Widow asked, a little skeptical.

"Look. It won't make anything better if we make it public that there's a terrorist threat involving Indians. Every place that has an Indian reservation would be targeted by hate groups. Plus, if we tell this community about the Ebola, everyone will panic, and the terrorists will be forced to release the virus. Then we'll have to mobilize the National Guard and quarantine a huge area. And even then, there's little we can do for them. A lot more people will die if we inform the public."

Shepard paused. "So go in there. Investigate. Find Jacobs for me. You don't need to interact with him. Just find him. We can go in after the storm and get him out. If he's dead, then get me a location or a name. Hitting one target will make it a lot better for everyone than hitting the whole community. We just need to either recover the case or destroy it."

"Do you have the manpower for an assault?"

Shepard switched the wipers to the highest setting, and the blades scraped across the glass, solving the problem for only about ten seconds. Then he said, "I have a small team waiting." He paused a beat and stared at the entrance to the reservation, coming up on the left.

He said, "Call me as soon as the snowstorm passes or when you know something. If I don't hear from you by morning, I'll have no choice but to have this place leveled. It's better to sacrifice a few lives over thousands."

He slowed the truck and turned without stopping onto the track that entered the reservation. They passed the sign and drove up to the community center. He pulled into the parking lot and made a U-turn, and pulled the truck right up to the curb. He clicked the button on his door's armrest, and Widow's door unlocked.

Shepard said, "Open the glove box."

Widow grabbed the handle to the glove box and popped it. The door fell open like a crocodile's mouth, and he saw a Walther P99 staring back at him. It was black with a matte finish. It had a manual decocker and rear slide serrations. The whole gun was nonslip, including the ergonomic grip. It was a small gun, a nine millimeter with a 7.1-inch length from nose to butt. The gun weighed a pound and a half, completely unloaded. It was a world-famous gun that had been trusted by European and Western military and police forces for decades. And there was one other factor that made this gun famous.

Widow picked up the gun and tilted it in his hand and said, "James Bond's gun? That's a little ironic."

"Take it. It's fully loaded, with fifteen rounds in the mag. You might need it."

So far, Widow had heard an insane story about Native American terrorists, undercover CIA operatives, and a deadly virus. Why shouldn't he have the same gun used by 007 in his hand? Widow took the gun and made sure the safety was on, and slipped it into his pocket. He didn't chamber it. He didn't think he'd need it.

Shepard said, "My number is programmed into the phone. Good luck."

Widow opened the door, climbed out into the snowy gloom, and watched as Shepard pulled away from the lot, drove off onto the road, and was gone from sight.

19

THE COMMUNITY CENTER was set way back from the complex and surrounded by trees. Off in the distance, a pair of sandhill cranes stood in the snow, taunting each other with calls. Maybe they were friends. Maybe not. Widow thought they would've flown south for the winter by now. Perhaps they still would. He wasn't one hundred percent sure of their migration patterns. Yellowstone wasn't exactly a mecca for birds migrating south. The high altitude and cold winters didn't make the park an optimal location for birds to migrate to. But there they were. Surely they would fly away before the storm progressed in this direction.

Widow moved his eyes from the birds and scanned the horizon. He could no longer see the luminous clouds from the north because the sky was now completely gray and white, and the snow had come on stronger than before, falling almost horizontal, like tilted rainfall.

He flicked his eyes back to the ground and saw a bear about a hundred yards away rearing up and staring at him from the tree line. It looked around casually, looked back at Widow, and then dashed off into the woods like it was more scared of him than he was of it.

Widow walked past the office to the community center and then around the corner of the building, making his way to the front entrance of the station house. He saw that both police cruisers were parked in the lot, and a green Jeep Cherokee. It was an older model—probably early 2000s. The tires were speckled with snow but relatively clear. Widow noticed his elongated reflection in the front windshield as he passed.

He walked to the front entrance, avoided the side one he entered when he was in handcuffs. He figured he was a member of the public now and not a prisoner. Best to use the public's entrance. He passed under a tin overhang, and there, etched on a double glass door, was the single word: "*Police*." The door squeaked as he pulled it open, and he heard a buzzer sound to show that a member of the public had entered the station house.

Inside the station, he was immediately greeted by a bulletin wall with various public service announcements on it—dates that the general store was closed, scheduled times for town hall meetings in the community center, and a new schedule for school buses that ran from the reservation to Tower Junction. Widow guessed there weren't enough kids on the reservation to warrant building a school of their own, although he suspected that most kids were home-schooled, anyway. The local public school was unlikely to teach tribal history and matters that concerned the community.

In the center of the bulletin board, there was a big black-and-white printed sheet that read, *"Warning! Snowstorm! Curfew in effect for nightfall!"*

It was dated with today's date.

To Widow's right, there was a small, cheap-looking desk with papers stacked on one side and nothing but a small computer on the other. A small, pale white woman sat behind it. She was young—probably early twenties. She wore glasses that blended right into her face and had long, curly red hair with dark streaks flowing through it. The woman was skinny in a bony way, like she could double as a teenage boy and fool most people.

She had a warm smile and flashed her white teeth at Widow as she said, "Can I help you?"

"I'm here to see Officer Red Cloud."

"Okay. Just a second. She just walked in, I think."

Widow glanced down at the girl's nameplate on her desk. It was Martha. Martha must've been from Tower Junction. He doubted there were any white people living on the reservation. Therefore, she probably commuted every day.

Martha stood up and walked behind a partition into the bullpen. The station house was a basic rectangle, leaving no more space beyond the partition for anything other than the bullpen, the chief's office, and the two empty cells at the rear, which he was all too familiar with.

Widow turned his back to the station house's interior and looked back at the door. He'd heard a car pull into the lot. The drive belt squealed like it was due to be changed, and then there was a loud whine from the brakes and the sound of chunks of snow being thrown away from the tires. He heard an emergency brake being pushed in and the *click* as it locked into place, then the sounds of two doors opening and closing. Moments later, a middle-aged man and woman walked into the station house. They smiled at Widow and waited behind him.

He said, "Good morning."

They said it back.

Widow heard a voice behind him ask, "What the hell are you doing back here?"

He turned to see Amita Red Cloud. She had a confused look on her face, rivaled only by the expression of fear he had seen on it the night before, when he had beaten up the two CIA agents.

Widow felt the Walther P99 in his pocket, poking him in the thigh. He tugged at the bottom of his shirt the best he could to keep the gun's small bulge hidden from view. The last thing he wanted to do was to let Amita know he'd returned with a gun.

In his back pocket was the satellite phone. Basic design. Basic package. It fit in his pocket with only the antenna poking out. He reminded himself not to sit on it. But he was sure that a sat phone coming from a CIA agent was probably built with durability in mind.

Amita repeated herself and said, "What the hell are you doing back here?"

"We gotta talk," he said.

"Come back," she said. And then she looked past him at the couple that had entered. She said, "I'm sorry. My dad's not here. He knows about your problem, and he'll be here shortly if you want to wait."

The wife nodded, but the husband looked angry at having to wait.

Widow didn't give them a second thought. He walked past Amita and disappeared behind the partition. He walked several paces back to the spot where they had all sat the night before and waited for her to join him.

"What the hell are you doing back here?" Amita asked a third time.

Widow remained standing. He said, "We need to talk. Your dad should know about this too."

"He'll be in shortly. What's going on?"

"Let's go into his office," Widow said, and walked to the chief's office. He didn't wait for permission. He needed to have a private conversation with Amita, and didn't want Martha to overhear.

They walked into the empty office. Widow turned to Amita and said, "This guy, Jacobs. Is he here?"

Amita turned pale. She said, "We went over that. What does this have to do with *your* being here?"

Widow stayed quiet. He studied her expression. She was lying. He knew it. But he didn't know what she was lying about. Did she know he was there? Did she know where he was?

Widow concluded it might be better to keep some of the truth to himself. The CIA, being so desperate that they had recruited a total stranger to help them locate a missing agent, sounded crazy. For another, Shepard had asked him not to tell anyone. That didn't really matter to Widow since he didn't owe allegiance to Shepard, the CIA, or anyone else. But he liked Amita Red Cloud and her father. And he didn't want to see anything bad happen to this community. The threat of bombing the reservation was preposterous. Widow knew that. But something about Shepard told him he wasn't lying about it as an option. Shepard was a serious guy. Widow had known spooks like him before.

"Widow! What the hell is going on?"

He trusted her. Sometimes the best way to earn trust was to give it first. He said, "The two guys who were up here. They aren't feds. Not technically. They're CIA agents."

Amita did a double take. She looked at Widow sideways. She asked, "Are you high?"

"I know it sounds crazy. But it explains how they got FBI badges."

"Why the hell would the CIA be here?"

Widow said, "Can't tell you the details."

"Don't even say that you'll have to kill me!" she said, and for the first time, a smile crept across her face, like she forgot who she was talking to.

Widow said, "Smiling looks much better on you than scowling."

"You're the reason I've been scowling."

Widow stayed quiet.

"You're serious about the CIA, aren't you?"

"That's what the guy told me."

"What guy?"

Widow explained to her about the diner and the guy with the scar. Before he could finish, her father walked into the station house with questions in his eyes but a hearty smile to greet his returned guest. Widow explained the entire story to both of them—all except the part about the Ebola virus. He figured it was best to leave that detail out. They had enough of an unbelievable story to swallow without the doomsday virus scenario tacked onto it. And although he wasn't supposed to tell anyone anything, he didn't work for the CIA. And he was pretty sure that neither of the Red Clouds would be involved in the crazy terrorist plot.

Amita said, "That's unbelievable."

"Well, it's what's happening. It explains why those two agents were here. Why they passed themselves off as feds."

"So, what do we do now?"

"They want me to find him. I need your help. We have little time."

Outside, the winds howled, and the sky clattered and rolled with the echo of a vengeful God. How only Mother Nature could sound. The storm was coming, and now was the time to look for Mike Jacobs.

20

WIDOW WASN'T GIVEN much time to find Jacobs. So far, there had been no sign of anyone getting sick. He remembered that there was an outbreak of Ebola in Texas recently. It had been all over the newspapers. They did not know how Ebola was transmitted. Nurses and doctors were getting sick and dying after caring for infected patients. No one seemed to have answers.

What Widow knew about Ebola was that it was fast, highly contagious, and deadly. If it had been released on the reservation, he was certain that everyone would know about it already. It wasn't too late.

Standing in the middle of the police station on the Red Rain Indian Reservation, Widow towered over Amita Red Cloud. But somehow, he felt in his bones that she was the one towering over him. Widow knew what it was like to be in the presence of a strong woman—his mother and his CO from Unit Ten, not to mention the many women he had served with. He didn't flinch or back down or feel intimidated by anyone—man or otherwise—but Amita made him reconsider this policy. If she told him to jump, he'd jump. He had no doubt about it.

Suddenly, his thoughts were interrupted.

In the distance, an alarm sounded, not an alarm from a car or a bank, but something different, something ominous and loud and booming. It was a siren.

Widow asked, "What's that?"

Amita said, "I don't know."

She looked past Widow's arms at her father, whose face had turned blue like he had been out in the freezing temperatures far too long. He said, "Tornado. The siren."

Widow asked, "In a snowstorm? Is that possible?"

Amita said, "It's unusual, but it happens."

"What do we do?"

"Brace ourselves and hope for the best."

They ran outside and looked at the skyline, searching for a twister.

At first, there was nothing. Nothing to the south. Nothing to the north. And nothing in either the west or the east.

Where is it? Widow thought.

The sky was filled with icy clouds and sparse snow, and gusting winds blew toward them from the blizzard, which was just over the horizon now. Giant black clouds circled around them like a flanking army. The mountain peaks were blurred and hidden behind a blanket of white. The trees from the forests faded from nearly the front all the way into the background, merging into a landscape of white and darkness and creating a cold, gray color that swelled.

Amita ran to her police cruiser, jacked open the door as fast as she could, and dumped down into her seat. She grabbed at the dashboard and pulled up the radio. She turned the ignition key to power the cruiser and called out across the radio channel.

Widow couldn't hear her from where he stood because of the distance and the gusts of wind. They had started out moderate only a moment ago but were gradually building up in speed and power and force. Within minutes, the United States flag, high on a thick metal flagpole in front of the community center, whipped and flapped like the sails on a sailboat far out at sea. The winds were changing and fore-telling of the approaching storm, and what they said was bad.

Red Cloud walked out near Widow, craned his neck, and used his left hand as a visor to protect his eyes, blocking out the snow that blew across the terrain in the wind. He looked across the sky in the opposite direction of his daughter and Widow.

Widow veered his eyesight left, covering the skyline, then traversed them to the right, scanning the rest of the sky and the land. That's when he saw it—a small but fast-moving twister. It zipped north and south like a creature that couldn't decide. He watched as snow lifted off the ground underneath it and filled the upper body with dark bursts of sleet and ice. The twister looked small, but Widow could tell it wasn't. It was an optical illusion, a trick of the sky. When he looked down at the base of the funnel, he saw that compared to the trees; the thing wasn't small at all, but massive.

The trees didn't come up out of the ground, but the branches were stripped of their bark.

Amita started shouting and pointing at the twister. "There!"

Widow shook off a sudden chill and glared at the monstrous twister carving a path toward him. At the base, Widow could see and hear trees cracking and the wind howling and swirling.

"Inside!" Amita shouted. "Take cover!"

They scampered back to the police station, Amita first and then Red Cloud. Widow waited until they went back in first, and then turned to take one last look at the twister that barreled right toward them. The sky was getting darker as the twister approached. The clouds above it swirled and looked like a whirlpool. Widow thought of a bathtub draining of water; only he was looking at it from the bottom and not the top. Then he turned and headed through the police station door, slamming it shut behind him.

"Do you have a basement?" he asked.

Amita said, "No. We aren't equipped for this kind of thing. Twisters are normally farther south. There used to be a shelter, but I can't remember what happened to it."

"What about the siren? You have that thing. So there must be a plan in place?"

She shook her head and said, "It's old. I've got no idea what we do."

Red Cloud signaled to everyone to head to the back hallway.

"The siren is before my time. Let's stay in here for now. It's probably the safest place. Not a lot of loose furniture."

Widow was the last to follow. The assistant, the civilians that were still there, Amita and her father, and Widow, all crammed together in the hallway with little space between them, mostly because the hallway wasn't long. Amita crowded close to Widow. Closer than he had expected, but he didn't react. He didn't want to scare her or signal to her he was uncomfortable with her closeness.

Three things happened suddenly and simultaneously. First, a loud, thunderous roar sounded outside, and the wail of the siren was gone. Second, the power in the police station crackled and short-circuited. Everything went black. And the third thing that happened was that Amita Red Cloud shivered, reached out, and grabbed hold of Widow's right hand—involuntarily. She squeezed it tight.

21

THE TWISTER reverberated and rumbled above the rooftop of the community center. The echo swelled through every chamber of the structure. Outside, the wind howled. Limbs and loose shingles clattered across the walls and the roof and crashed into the police cruisers and the cars in the lot. The lights were out, and the station was black as night. There were no windows in the hall.

Widow felt Amita's hand squeeze his own, and he heard her breathing like an engine humming at the starting line, waiting for the racing flag, waiting to speed up.

The twister lived for all of ten minutes, but in that small amount of time, it caused a lot of cosmetic damage, at the very least. Widow knew that for sure. They all did. No way was the sound and fury of the thing capable of doing anything less.

After the sounds died down to just the howl of the wind, Amita let go of his hand and moved down the hall to check out the station. Widow followed her, but stayed a giant step behind, giving her space. Before they made it to the door of the station, they saw a beam of light shining into the station. The light came from where the door used to be. It was dim, but it lit up the room. The heavy orange door to the station house had been ripped off at the hinges. The sound had probably been loud but was masked by the volume of the twister. From where they stood, there was no sign of the door, only the broken metal hinges that swiveled and dangled from the doorframe.

Amita said, "Shit."

Widow nodded and stayed quiet. He walked past her and out the door and gazed out upon the scene in front of him.

The scene outside wasn't as bad as it had sounded. Part of the reason for that was that the entire community had already expected a snowstorm that would last overnight to sweep through. So they had already prepared. Many of the people had closed their shutters and moved in with their relatives who had houses and basements and generators.

"We have to open the community center as a shelter for people who need it," Red Cloud said from behind Widow.

Widow turned and saw him standing just outside the doorway. Amita was off to the south a bit, looking over the horizon and the destruction. The twister had died away. It came on fast and had died away fast. There was no sign of it anywhere. One minute, it had been a harbinger of destruction, and the next, it had evaporated into thin air.

"Let's start now. We won't get a better chance. The snowstorm will get worse," Red Cloud said.

Widow nodded. He looked at the sky again and saw that the white grayness was less than a mile away. The fast-paced snowstorm caused Widow some concern because Shepard had said that after the blizzard passed, they needed results. And the faster the storm passed over them, the faster Shepard would keep his promise.

Widow walked over to Amita and said, "We'd better take this time to look for Jacobs. It'll be impossible when the storm hits harder."

Amita nodded in agreement. Then she went over to her father and explained. Widow couldn't hear them, but he saw Chief Red Cloud shake his head in disagreement.

Amita came back and said, "My dad wants us to help with the shelter first. He said our priority is the community center, even though I told him how important it is. He's calling a town meeting. Half of the community will head this way and stay in the community center. So after we get them in, we'll let you ask about Jacobs. Maybe one of them will know something. Okay?"

"That'll have to do," Widow said. Then he added, "What can I do to help?"

Amita sensed his disappointment and said, "How about this? We need to clear the road of falling debris as fast as possible. You and I can go out in the cruiser and do that." She stopped talking and looked up at the skyline again. Then she said, "Looks like we have less than an hour. Let's get moving, and while we're out, we'll look for any sign of Jacobs. Deal?"

"You won't mind?"

"I have a job to do. Doesn't matter my history with him. I tried to help those federal agents or CIA or whatever. And I'll help you. Sounds like if we don't, they'll only return and cause more problems. And we got other things to deal with."

Widow stayed quiet and headed for the car. He didn't wait for her. Amita read nothing into it. He knew she wouldn't. She was a hard woman, hard as they come. She followed suit and followed him to the police cruiser.

The door to Amita's car was undamaged and was still open from when the tornado had struck. The seat belt warning was beeping. Widow sat down in the passenger seat. He saw she had left the keys dangling in the ignition. Amita plopped down in the driver's seat and shut the door. She fired up the engine and hit the gas. The car swerved around in a circle and then moved forward as she released the gas a little. The tires peeled up snow, and a small tree limb dragged behind for four or five feet until it let go, releasing itself back into the parking lot.

The cruiser was slow-going on the snow-covered roads until they reached the main street, where its tires dug through the snow and met concrete. Then the car drove the way it was intended, and they headed north at a medium pace.

22

WIDOW ASKED, "What exactly are we doing?"

"I told you. Clearing debris."

"No, I mean, what's our priority? Any debris or major stuff?"

"We're looking for big things. Major damage. People in trouble. Roadblocks. That sort of thing," Amita said.

Widow nodded. He knew it was her job. Although he wanted to help, he thought about the missing CIA agent and the terrorists on her reservation. He thought, too, about Shepard's threat that the CIA would do anything to prevent a weaponized Ebola attack. Widow didn't have to wonder about what "anything" meant. He knew it meant something bad, something irreversible.

"Don't worry. We're going to look around. Later, when everyone is in the community center, you can ask if anyone has seen him. I want to help, Widow."

"Thank you. It's a matter of national security, which means we need to find him. If we don't, it'll be bad for you and bad for Red Rain Indian Reservation."

Amita paused a beat and then asked, "What do you mean, bad for us?"

Widow stayed quiet.

"Widow, tell me. What's going to happen if we don't find him?"

"I honestly don't know, but I fear it'll be bad. The CIA isn't supposed to be here. They're here because of suspected terrorist activities. They aren't going to go away until they get what they want. And I'm afraid it'll be at any cost. And that the reservation will be the one to pay the price."

"What cost do you mean?"

"I don't know."

"Do you think they'll raid the reservation? Take everyone prisoner until they find Jacobs?"

"I worry that it's far worse than that," Widow said. He paused, then he said, "Later. Okay? Let's talk about it later. Let's just worry about finding him."

Amita said, "Okay."

They drove on, taking it slow, taking it easy.

The cruiser drove over the road with no problem. They drove on until they came to an obvious path that the twister had made. Debris littered the ground. Amita switched on the light bar. Blue lights flashed across the terrain. Under the darkening sky, the lights bounced off treetops and reflected from the windows of nearby houses and low mobile homes strung together in tight, unorganized sequences.

Widow let his eyes trace the area, looking for damage from the tornado. Amita peered around, doing the same, looking one way and then the other.

She said, "Look there."

Widow followed her gaze. He saw several mobile homes— some flipped or turned over, and some completely torn apart. Standing in a small crowd around building shrapnel were the former residents of the destroyed homes.

Amita said, "We'd better go look."

She turned the wheel, and the cruiser turned and dipped over the snow. They drove off the road and onto the flat ground toward the people. They pulled up a few feet from the crowd and saw Henry Little among them.

Amita Red Cloud stomped on the parking brake, threw open the door, and got out without bothering to close it. She propped one foot up on the interior of the doorframe and leaned up over the roof. She called out across the top. "Is everyone okay?"

Henry Little looked back at her and said, "Everyone's good."

Amita climbed out all the way and signaled to Widow to follow her. He got out of the car and shut his door. Widow could feel his feet sink farther down into the already fallen snow. The temperature had dropped steadily, but it hadn't really affected him too much up to this point, but now he felt the cold, like icy nails were poking his skin.

Amita looked back over her shoulder and saw Widow trailing behind, shivering a little as he walked. She stopped walking and stood close to Henry Little.

"What are you all doing out here?"

Henry Little said, "We're trying to help Samantha search for pictures of her husband." Then he stopped and turned to gaze at Widow. Little's face was long with pronounced eyebrows. He looked Widow up and down and then up again. He said, "Her husband died in Afghanistan. She just received the phone call today."

Widow stayed quiet. Afghanistan was a place he knew, but was fortunate not to have spent too much time in. He had never been stationed there, not on land.

Little moved closer to him. Before, Widow had thought that Little was a giant. But now, he retracted that because Little wasn't a giant—he was a leviathan.

"He fought in the Army. Now, he's dead. And now she has lost the small amount of home that *your* government allows her to have."

Widow stared at him, didn't respond.

"Okay. That's enough, Henry. Come on. He has nothing to do with any of that nonsense," Amita said.

Little ignored her and continued moving toward him. Widow could smell alcohol on his breath. Widow thought about what a man who knew there was a major storm approaching would do if he were locked in his house. What would he do? He'd drink.

Widow didn't feel he should judge or say anything about it. But then Little did something Widow didn't like—he poked Widow's chest.

Widow said, "Sorry about your friend. But it's no more my government than it is yours. And I don't make decisions about your land. I don't make decisions about anything. I'm just a guy."

"Are you not a white man?"

Widow said, "Obviously, I'm white. And I was in the military. But I've played no role in anything that affects you."

Little asked, "Military? You look Army."

"Navy."

Little poked Widow again. Amita stepped between them and said, "Henry! That's enough!"

He pushed past her and poked again.

Widow said, "Don't poke me."

Little came close and raised his hand up in the air and held it there like a major debate was taking place in his head.

Amita said, "Henry, stop! This makes you look like a jerk!"

Henry Little backed down, and Widow sighed to himself in relief. He didn't want to hurt an old Native American in front of Amita. Not only that, but he also didn't disagree.

Amita said, "We're out here to tell everyone to head to the community center. We'll be safer buckled down there for the night. It's stocked with supplies and sleeping bags. Spread the word."

Henry nodded, said, "Yeah. Okay. I'll tell people. We'll all be there. Now they have nowhere else to go."

Widow felt bad about their homes but said nothing about it. He said, "Amita, we'd better get moving."

They returned to the car and drove about as far as they could before the snow started. Within a matter of moments, it had turned to hard wind and then harder snow.

Amita said, "This is insane. I've lived through storms before, but I've never seen it come on so fast."

Widow stared out the window and shrugged. He had never seen this much snow, and it had only been coming down for a few minutes.

Amita said, "We'd better go back."

These were words Widow didn't like hearing. He never went back. Going back wasn't something in his nature. Going forward was his thing. But he nodded. Amita backed the car up and K-turned and headed back to the community center.

23

VIOLENT WINDS BLASTED through the snow-covered streets and the quieted buildings of Red Rain Indian Reservation. A stop sign hung broken and flapped in the wind like a metal flag. Shingles on a nearby roof shuddered and rattled, on the verge of coming off. The old wood of the houses moaned in the storm's vehemence. Some trees bent while others stood strong, their bases secured by three feet of snow. Ice ricocheted off the old telephone poles, and wooden slivers flew off the sides like bark peeling off a tree. The snow didn't fall—it shot and darted across the sky, assaulting the landscape. One temporarily abandoned home had three broken windows because the inhabitants had forgotten to close the shutters. By the time they returned, the place would be filled with snow.

This continued for about seventy-five minutes, and then, suddenly, the storm subsided. It wound down to a milder version of itself, but it was far from over. On a radar screen, the storm would've covered half the map of Northern

Wyoming. The sudden calm was merely a pocket in the bigger system, a break from the relentless bombardment.

Down the main street, in the community center, Widow leaned against the back wall of the main chamber. He faced a crowd of locals, most of them with their backs turned. They faced each other and chatted. The low rumble of their voices hummed through the chamber like a church after Mass, when everyone stirs and gathers their belongings, saying hello to members of their congregation. Most of the townspeople were over the age of fifty. There were some small children and a handful of young adults.

No one paid any attention to Widow.

From across the room, Amita Red Cloud looked over at him and then turned back to her father. They spoke for a few minutes. Then she turned and walked toward Widow.

She stopped in front of him and looked up, cocking her head back. She said, "Tell them. My dad is going to get their attention. He wants you to tell them about Jacobs. It's the fastest way to find him. Ask if they've seen him. Someone is bound to know something."

Widow said, "I'm not good in front of crowds."

Amita cracked a smile, and then she said, "I can't believe you're scared of them."

Widow shrugged. "Not afraid. I just have little experience in public speaking."

"Nervous?"

"No."

"Okay then, so get ready."

Chief Red Cloud waved his hands in the air, and the crowd turned and gave him their attention.

He said, "Thanks for your attention. I know that everyone here is in some serious worry about this storm and your homes. I'm glad you heeded our warnings and came to us here. Every year, we get a blizzard or two. This is the worst one I can recall, but we're still safe here. Together."

He walked toward Widow.

"Now I know that many of you are dealin' with the loss of your property because of the twister. Right now, there's nothing we can do about that. Right now, we've got an important matter that must be dealt with. Unfortunately, it's sensitive. I'm asking for your help. Each of you, turn your attention to Mr. Widow. He'll explain."

The crowd turned like one being. There were less than a hundred faces, but over fifty. Widow wasn't sure because when they all stared at him, their faces blurred together. Being the center of attention wasn't something he liked. It made him feel like an outcast because he was so different from everyone else.

Widow swallowed and said, "There are dangerous men among you." No transition. No preparation. He just said it like it was.

The crowd froze and stared at him.

He said, "There's a missing federal agent. It's complicated. We need to find him."

Amita stepped forward and said, "Some of you know him. His name is Mike Jacobs. Does anyone know where he is? Has anyone seen him?"

No one stepped up. No one made a sound.

Widow waited and scanned the sea of faces, but there wasn't a glimmer of recognition in any of them. There were residents missing from the congregation of people. Widow wondered if Jacobs was with one of them. Perhaps people in terrorist cells would remain in their houses—it would make sense. Terrorists live among us, unsuspected, but they were still usually people on the fringes. Hard to hide what you were doing in plain sight. Especially in a small, tight community like this one. Widow had grown up in a small community, and he knew what it was like to stay hidden from public view. In a small town, everyone knew your business.

Widow looked at Amita and shook his head. No one in the room knew anything about Jacobs. Widow doubted that any of them would help, even if they knew. Jacobs was like a needle in a haystack.

Amita approached Widow and said, "Some people aren't here."

"I figured."

"Some live far from the center of town."

"I figured that too. I can't blame them for wanting to stay with their property."

Amita said, "Widow, Mike Jacobs's family home is one of those places. It's on the outskirts. His family sold it to an older man named Sean Gareth."

"Gareth?" Widow asked.

"He's a white man. No one minds him because he keeps to himself. Hardly ever see him in town. Henry usually travels out to his house and delivers supplies once a week. They're friends. They play poker. Everyone knows about it because Henry usually hates white people, as you saw. But he and Gareth are friends."

Widow looked at her. He felt the P99 shift in his pocket. Then he said, "That might be a good place to look."

24

THE SMALL BOY had been told to run.

And that was what he'd done. He ran as hard and fast as he could through the snow and the trees and the broken limbs. He heard loud noises behind him. Some of them he didn't recognize. Loud engine sounds. But some he knew. He heard gunshots. He knew those. The boy had seen plenty of movies, bad movies, movies his parents hadn't wanted him to watch. He didn't really understand what was going on. The boy only wanted to go home. He wanted to see his parents again. He wondered why he hadn't seen them.

The man had taken him away from the bad men. He understood bad men. He had seen them in movies, too.

What he had never seen was real-life violence. Not like tonight. Tonight, he had seen a man on fire.

The boy had walked close to him in the freezing snow. He had watched the man combust and then flail around like a chicken with his head cut off. The man had stopped and dropped to his knees, and then he'd dropped flat onto the ground and continued to blaze. The boy had stared at him, not sure what to do.

There was a lot of noise. Gunshots. An explosion. Crackling fire. A dog barking in the distance. Voices yelling.

The man screamed at him to run. Run. So the small boy turned and ran. He didn't want to because it was cold. Not near the fiery man. Near him, it was warm. But he had to run. He had to listen to the man he had arrived with.

Before he ran, he saw an object on the ground. He wasn't sure what it was. But it blinked. It was small and box-shaped. He picked it up. He saw the blinking light. And he slipped it into his coat pocket.

"Run!" the man screamed again.

The small boy ran into the forest and over the thick snow, and away from the nightmarish sounds.

25

WIDOW WONDERED where the hell Mike Jacobs was and how the hell he was going to find him. It looked like they would have to go out into the snowstorm to search for him. Door to door. House to house. But maybe not everywhere. The best bet would be to start way out where Jacobs's family house had been. Maybe he had escaped the terrorist cell and was hiding out. Maybe he was holed up, waiting for the storm to pass so he could get in touch with Shepard.

Just then, two unexpected things happened.

The community center and all the people inside seemed to freeze as the lights flickered and the power went out again. The room went black. A hum could be heard surging through the circuitry as the emergency backup lights kicked on. The room filled with an unnatural feeling when the lights shot on. They were bright. The white light filled the room like a blast from the sun.

The second thing to happen was that the door to the community center burst open. The power from the reservation was out everywhere, and the blackness seemed to seep in with the open door.

Widow saw him first. A small Mexican boy stumbled in. He was covered in muddy snow, ice, and frost. The kid shivered, even though he wore a thick winter coat that was too big for him. He came in and fell to the floor right in the doorway. The door slowly closed and stopped against his body. Widow, as well as some people who were closer, scrambled toward him.

Widow pushed through the crowd of people, ignored the mumbling. He grabbed at the boy's head and pulled him up. The boy was breathing, which relieved Widow and Amita. She had pushed through behind Widow, using him as a forward blocker.

She said, "I don't know him. Does anyone know him?"

She looked around the crowd of people. Everyone shrugged slowly, one after the other, like a camera was panning around the room.

She asked, "Who is he? Where did he come from?"

Widow stayed quiet.

26

THE SMALL BOY woke up lying on a cot in a strange place. He wasn't sure where he was or how he had gotten there. He knew he had been out in the cold, walking and freezing. A storm had come and swallowed him up. He had been scared, but now he felt safe.

Standing over him was the biggest man he'd ever seen. He had a ridged brow and a hard face. Deep ice-blue eyes. Short, thick, dark hair. The man had dark-colored tattoos peeking out from the bottom of his sleeves. He had broad shoulders and an enormous chest. He looked like one of those scary monster men from the movies on the channel his mom said he wasn't allowed to watch. "Grown-up movies," she called them. Only she said it in Spanish. He knew a little English from watching those movies. He knew some bad words, too.

Even though he was scary, the giant man didn't scare him because he had a friendly way about him. He seemed warm, and he was friendly to the boy. He had put blankets on him and made sure he was comfortable. Plus, there was a Mexican police officer with him. At least she looked Mexican. She had dark hair and brown eyes. But she differed from the Mexicans he had known his entire life. And she spoke no Spanish, only English.

They waited for him to get his breath and his warmth back.

The woman said, "Where are you from, honey?"

He didn't answer. His English was broken, but he understood they wanted to know where he lived.

The monster man asked, "Where are your parents?"

He said nothing.

The monster man knelt beside him and asked, "Do you remember anything? Your name?"

His face scrunched in a funny expression. Then he said, "Loud. Engine. Vrrrrm. Vrrrrm."

The monster man looked at the policewoman.

She knelt closer and asked, "You heard a loud noise? Like an engine?"

He said, "Copper. Copper. Boom."

"Boom?" the policewoman asked.

Then the monster man folded his hands together and separated them in a violent, swift movement like an explosion. He knew what the man was asking and nodded.

He said, "'Plosion."

The woman police officer asked, "Explosion? Where?"

"Where did you hear the explosion?" the monster man asked.

The boy said, "Mi amigo. He protect. He protect."

"Amigo?" the policewoman asked. "Where's he now?"

The boy swallowed and said, "Él está muerto."

The monster man looked at the cop and said, "He's dead."

"Maybe it was his father?" she replied in a hushed voice.

The monster man asked, "What's his name?"

He said, "Miguel." Then he paused and said, "Pero algunos chicos le llamaban Jacobs."

The policewoman froze. She turned to the monster man and asked, "What did he say?"

The monster man must've understood Spanish because he translated. He said, "But some guys call him Jacobs. He's talking about Mike Jacobs, our missing agent."

27

WIDOW EYEBALLED the snowy terrain from the community center's front windows. The local buildings and signs were black from the power outage. The stars in the sky shone through a significant break in the cloud cover, brightening the landscape, bringing a false sense of calmness.

Widow saw the snow, the cars, and the power lines—all quiet.

A major pocket in the center of the storm blew over them, making it seem like it was over.

Red Cloud said, "It's not over. It's just beginning."

"You think?" Widow asked.

"Definitely. Besides living here for fifty-five years and knowing my homeland, my arthritis never lies.

Widow was silent.

"Plus," he had added, "the guy on the radio said there was more."

The main street was far too snowed over to navigate by car. Widow couldn't see any of the concrete, only the whiteness of the snow that covered it.

Amita came up behind Widow and tapped him on the back of the shoulder. Red Cloud walked away, leaving them in private.

Widow looked back at her. She held out a police coat with the tribal police patches on it and a nice, thick lining made of wool that had aged to a sandy color from its original white.

She handed it to him along with a brown wool cap.

She said, "These are my father's. Came with the job. Only they're two sizes too big for him. They should fit you. Wear them. It's far too cold out there for you to just wear that."

"Thank you."

He grabbed the coat and the cap, draped the coat over his left forearm, and held the cap in his left hand. He turned and looked down at her.

"Let's get out there," said Amita. "If the boy was talking about an explosion, there could be people hurt. We need to check it out."

Widow said, "I agree. We'd better get going now. This weather won't stay quiet all night. We should start at the Jacobses' family house. You said he had a house somewhere?"

Amita said, "It's up on the mountain, far away from almost everyone else."

Widow said, "Then that's where we should go. If he's in trouble, he might be holed up there."

"What about this kid? How does he fit in?"

Widow said, "I have no idea. But we aren't going to get answers from him. We need to find Jacobs."

"Agreed."

"How do we get up there?"

Amita said, "Horseback is the only way."

"What about snowmobile?"

"No snowmobile. The road is the only way smooth enough for a snowmobile. Snowmobiles can traverse rugged terrain, but not like this. Trust me. Horseback is the best way."

Widow shrugged. "Sounds good. Let's get going. Where do we get horses?"

"The police department has some on standby. They belong to us, but a local rancher stables them."

"How far?"

"In this snow, it's going to be a good hike. I've radioed ahead and told the rancher. He'll have the horses saddled and ready to ride by the time we walk there. It'll take us nearly an hour."

Widow stayed quiet. He nodded.

Amita said, "Also, my father wants me to give you a gun. We'll be up there alone. He has to stay behind. He's the only other officer. It'll just be the two of us. He'll feel better if we're both armed. You can shoot straight, right?"

Widow brandished the Walther P99 and showed it to her.

"Where the hell did you get that?"

Widow said, "The CIA agent gave it to me."

"Is that the James Bond gun?"

"It is," Widow said.

"That's a peashooter."

"Hey, it's not that bad. Not as bad as the smaller Sean Connery version from nineteen sixty-whatever. This one has plenty of stopping power. Besides, if it's good enough for 007, then it's good enough for me."

"Whatever. Does it work?"

Widow said, "I haven't field-tested it."

"Better check it. Always check your weapon first. Don't use an untested gun."

"I know, I know. Let's go outside. I'll try it."

They walked to the outer doors, and Widow stopped and slipped the Walther P99 back into the front pocket in his trousers. He pulled out the cap from the inner pocket of the police coat, opened it up, and slipped it on. It was a decent fit. The lining was nice and thick and warm. The sleeves were a little too short, but he had expected that. There weren't a lot of clothes in the world that fit his arms. Not in the greater sense of the world's size and population, but like when he thought about how many clothes were out there in the world. The world had seven billion people living in it, and most of them had over one set of clothes. Some had hundreds of items—even thousands. Widow wasn't sure. He could imagine some celebrities owning maybe even a million sets of clothes, some rich old actress collecting clothes her entire career. She could have mansions full of clothes.

Regardless, he was grateful to have the warm police coat, even if it was a little short in the sleeves.

He followed Amita out into the snow. They walked to the rear of her police cruiser and stopped at the trunk. She pointed to a thick wooden fence post at the rear of the community center. It was about sixty yards away.

She said, "There. Let's go there."

They walked through the snow and closer to the fence. When they got twenty-five yards from it, she stopped and pointed at it.

"Shoot that."

Widow studied the fence and saw older bullet holes in the hoary wood. Obviously, something Amita used regularly for target practice. He wasn't sure about where she had imagined a bad guy to be, but if it was the obvious place, the spot where a bad guy could stand clearly, then she was a decent shot. There was one spot with multiple bullet holes clustered around it, like that was where she imagined a heart to be.

Widow pulled the P99 out of his pocket and rechecked the magazine. He loaded it and racked the slide, chambering a bullet. Widow looked down the sights at the fence, checking the accuracy. He steadied the gun with one hand and held it out with the other, right index finger in the trigger housing over the trigger. He didn't need to brace himself. The P99 was a decent handgun. No reason to worry about muzzle climb or kick, as neither was really a factor with this gun. It was a standard nine-millimeter piece—lightweight and compact.

He breathed in and squeezed the trigger. The bullet rocketed through the air, and the gunshot rang out and echoed through the trees and across the tops of the nearby buildings. Widow fired only once. He tilted his head and looked beyond the barrel at the target. His shot had plugged a standard nine-millimeter hole into the wood.

Amita giggled.

He turned and looked at her and asked, "What?"

"You call that shooting?"

"I hit it."

"Your shot is six inches from mine, which is obviously the center mass if that were a man."

Widow said, "I didn't realize you wanted me to aim. I thought we were just testing the gun."

Amita said, "Whatever. Try it again."

"Better that I don't. The gun only holds fifteen rounds in the magazine. That was one. With it chambered, there are only fourteen left. I might need them."

Amita shrugged and then said, "Okay. Let's go."

Widow pocketed the P99, but this time, he slipped it into the coat pocket. There was plenty of room in there, more than in his pants pocket.

They faced east and walked beyond the community center, along the road for a while, and then they turned north. Amita led the way. She walked through the snow with ease. Widow took slower steps, partially because he was heavy, and his feet kept sinking into the snow. He felt like the tin man after a long period of being rusted over and not having any oil. If only there was an oil can for him to use. He wondered how Amita walked so gracefully across the snowy ground, but maybe it was because she was lighter. Maybe her boots had special winter soles. Or maybe it was because she was used to it. At any rate, she was much faster and a lot more graceful than he was.

They walked for thirty-nine minutes, crossing hilly terrain and walking between some of the thickest trees Widow had ever seen—in real life or on TV or on the internet or in magazines.

Amita twisted and bobbed and walked through a clearing. Widow followed. They crossed over a snow-filled ditch, and Widow saw a long wooden fence made of two parallel posts, just like the ones he had seen in old Western movies on a cattle ranch. Then he saw a large brick house with snow-covered windows and smoke coming out of a chimney. He heard sounds coming from the house. Television sounds. This guy still had power. As Widow neared the house, he saw and heard a generator running under a canopy at the rear of the house.

Amita pointed beyond the house to a stable. She said, "There."

Widow saw the rancher near the stable. He was a short guy with features similar to Henry Little's; only he was actually little. Same facial structure, like they could have been brothers or cousins with similar genes. The guy was smoking a cigarette and standing in a large doorway that led into the stable. He watched them approach, took one last big puff from his cigarette, and flicked it into the snow. Widow guessed it made little sense to put it out first. Snow wasn't flammable. The cigarette landed three feet from the guy. The flame died in a matter of seconds, partially because of the snow and partially because it nearly froze over.

That was the first time Widow realized just how warm his new coat was. He felt much more comfortable than before. He was glad to have it.

Amita stopped and talked to the rancher for a moment. Widow shook his hand, and they introduced themselves. The rancher showed them to the horses. There were three of them, two large black ones and one pinto with white-and-black coloring.

Amita asked, "Why are three saddled up?"

The rancher said, "Your father said you might need backup."

"Backup?"

"You know, like reinforcements. He said you guys were looking for a dangerous man."

"No. We don't need that. You stay behind. We can handle it."

The rancher said, "But your father said—"

"I don't care what he said. Tell him I made you stay behind. Or tell him you went and everything was kosher. I don't care, but you can't go."

"But what about the horses? The terrain?"

Amita rolled her eyes and said, "We'll be fine. I've ridden horses before, and I've lived here my whole life. You know that. No more arguing. We need to get going."

The rancher shrugged and said nothing else about it. He turned and pointed at the horses and said, "You know what to do."

Then he turned and strolled off, back toward the house. He looked defeated and let down, like a big kid not getting his way. Maybe he had wanted to go. A dangerous mission probably sounded exciting to him. Maybe he had no visitors and not much excitement in his life. And he had jumped at the opportunity to do her father a favor and watch over her on this excursion.

But Amita was right. As a police officer, it was her duty to protect the citizens of the reservation. She had made the right call. Widow didn't matter to her. He wasn't a part of the reservation, not a part of her ilk.

Widow didn't know what to expect when they got to the Jacobses' family house. Maybe they'd find the CIA agent, and maybe they wouldn't. Maybe they'd find danger, and maybe they wouldn't. The only thing Widow felt pretty positive about was that they would not find Jacobs playing hooky, which was the best-case scenario. But playing hooky was something that high school kids or people with regular jobs did. Sometimes cops and sometimes even sailors, but never government agents of the most elite secret agency in the world. CIA recruits might have been guilty of playing hooky, but they probably never made it to their second day as a recruit, much less a regular field agent. This wasn't kid stuff.

Amita led Widow to the horses, grabbed the reins on the pinto, and tugged on them. The horse huffed a low, rumbling sound and followed her lead out of the stable. Then she looked at Widow and said, "Grab the other one."

Widow assumed it didn't matter which horse, and he reached for the younger-looking one and followed Amita's lead. They walked out of the stable and followed the snowy path that led off into the trees and up the nearest peak.

Amita placed her left foot in the stirrup and pulled herself up onto the horse. Then she looked at Widow, who seemed clueless. She asked, "Ever ridden a horse?"

"No. Not really. I get the mechanics of it."

She said, "Don't be scared. Just do what I did. Get up there."

Widow stared at the animal, didn't move.

"Well, come on. We don't have all day. Maybe another two hours by the looks of the weather, and it's going to take us forty-five minutes of that time just to get to Jacobs's house."

Widow shrugged, then grabbed the saddle horn with one hand and hauled himself up onto the horse. He pivoted one foot and launched himself over the top of the saddle. He righted himself until he was comfortable, shifting left, shifting right. The animal moved and shifted to counter his weight.

Amita laughed and smiled and made a wisecrack, but she just exhaled instead and shook her head. Then she kicked the horse gently and steered it off toward the path.

She called back to him, "Come on, city boy. Giddyap."

Widow smiled. *City boy?* Not many people had ever called him that before.

The two of them crisscrossed through the ranch and into the trees. It took only about five minutes before they saw the first dead body.

28

IT WAS A DEAD DOG.

Widow and Amita stared down from their perches on their horses at a half-frozen, dead Siberian husky. Its tongue had rolled out of its mouth and across its sharp canines. The tongue was a light-blue color. Widow guessed the poor animal hadn't been dead very long. Less than two hours probably, mainly because it wasn't covered in snow yet; but then again, the snow had slowed, and the heavy tree branches above could've acted as an umbrella. Also, the cold weather could have preserved it or made it look older than it was by turning parts of it blue.

Amita asked, "What happened to it?"

Widow said, "There's blood all underneath its hindquarters. See?"

He pointed at a deep black spot that sank way down in the snow.

He spun slowly on his saddle and stumbled about, and finally slid off the horse. Amita followed suit. Only she did it with the grace of an experienced rider—in one fluid action. They huddled around the dead dog.

Widow asked, "Recognize it?"

Amita said, "I don't know. There are lots of them around here. Popular dog."

Widow nodded. He looked at the neck and said, "No tag."

"Hard to keep a collar on a husky. They chew them off. They won't stop until they get out of it."

"I never owned one."

Amita said, "No smell either."

"Too cold. The snow buried part of the dog and is probably masking the smell. I'm guessing he's been dead for less than two hours."

"So, what killed it?"

Widow gripped the dog's legs. Left hand, front leg. Right hand, back leg. Then he heaved and pulled the corpse out of the snow and peeked underneath.

That was when the smell hit them like a blast of rotten air. It wasn't a lingering stench, but it had been covered for a long time and came out in one big puff. Widow leaned back and let the smell waft by, while Amita took a giant step back and took in a deep breath from the clean air, away from the dead dog.

She repeated, "What killed it?"

Widow looked down at a gaping hole in the right side of the animal, just above its back leg. He said, "Gunshot."

29

THE TOPOGRAPHY through the trees was a gradual rise from a hilly area that eventually turned into a rocky one. The trees became sparser, and the temperature dropped slightly —the higher elevation combined with the gap in the storm closing and becoming blizzard weather again.

They rode the horses at a fast pace every chance they got, but mostly, the trip was made at a fast walk. The flatter land had too many trees, and the rocky land was too rugged and steep to full-on gallop with a horse. And all of it was too snowy to force the animals to run. So it took about forty-five minutes, as Amita had predicted.

During the whole trek, both of them wondered who would shoot a husky.

What kind of man would do that? Widow thought.

He had always had a soft spot for dogs. He sometimes thought about getting one. A companion for the road might be a nice change.

The other thing running through his mind was that for the entire way so far, there had been a long streak in the snow, a depression, followed by paw prints. The prints were shallow and spread farther apart at first, but then they became deep and steady, plainly showing the dog's march to death as it slowed to a final crawl—the dog's last walk in reverse.

The strange thing was that it looked like the dog had been dragging something.

The other obvious thing was the long streak of blood that eventually turned into droplets, like the dog had been shot, and as it went farther, there was less blood to bleed out. And the farther they rode on horseback, the more Widow wondered what the dog had dragged for such a long distance—and where that thing was now.

Amita spoke first about it. She said, "That dog dragged something through the snow and then died. It must've been something important. What would a dog with a bullet above its leg drag all this way?"

Widow said, "I've got no idea."

30

CHIEF RED CLOUD watched the boy from near the window. Then he stared back outside and watched the horizon for Amita. He wanted her to come back safely. Something about this whole situation didn't sit right with him. Why would the CIA be interested in Mike Jacobs? As far as he remembered, Jacobs was a not-so-special kid who had always had dreams of leaving his home. As far as Red Cloud was concerned, the only thing Jacobs ever did right was to leave his daughter so she could live her life without him. And thank God he had never gotten her pregnant. For that, Amita's father was grateful. Jacobs would've abandoned her to raise the kid on her own. Red Cloud did not doubt that.

He looked back at the boy. The boy sat upright and looked around. No one was paying attention to him anymore. The adults were all preoccupied, talking in whispers. Amita's father watched as the young boy glanced around. It was as if he was making sure no one saw him. Then he reached into his coat pocket and pulled something out, something small and dark. The boy shifted in his seat and fumbled with the object some more. Amita's father turned fully toward him and walked over. He got about halfway there and saw that the boy was playing with a device with a blinking red light. It blinked and blinked like a light on a plane.

Red Cloud walked closer. It was a peculiar thing for a child to have. He surveyed it. The device looked strange. It didn't look like a toy. It looked high tech, like it was military.

31

THE DARKNESS SURROUNDED them for most of the journey up the mountain until they got to the top of a hill. Then everything was red, like the sky just before the sun sinks below the western horizon. They couldn't see the sky though, because it was filled with smoke. The smoke was thick and dark. Widow knew that just above the smoke were more clouds full of harsh snow, ready to pour down at any second.

Widow stood in his stirrups and gazed through the trees. Then he saw it. Not too far off. There was a smoldering structure. A torrent of fire raged, exhaling dark smoke into the sky. Flames seethed and roared. The good news was that the only thing on fire was the structure. The trees were too far away, and the ground was covered in snow. Soon the storm would return to put the flames out.

"Fire," Widow said. "Just over there. It looks like a house. Explosion maybe."

Amita said, "Oh Jesus! That's Mike's house. Mr. Gareth!" She kicked the pinto and shouted, "Yaw!"

The animal made a noise and picked up her pace, and Widow watched as Amita carelessly galloped past the trees, heading toward the house.

Widow kicked his horse in the rear and followed behind. He got to the house only a moment after she did, but he might as well have been a half hour after because she was already off her horse and standing over a dead body. It was turned over, and she was kneeling down beside it. It looked like she had tried to resuscitate the person and failed. Her shoulders were hunched, and her head was buried in her hands.

Widow walked up behind her. The flames crackled, and the remaining section of the house crumbled and collapsed to the ground.

"Who is it?" Widow asked.

Amita looked back up at him with an expression Widow had seen before on other people. It wasn't grief or sorrow but sadness, because it was such a small community. They were all like an extended family, even the white man who lived on the edge of the reservation.

"It's Mr. Gareth," she said. "He's dead."

Widow nodded, studied the terrain. There was another corpse about forty feet from the house.

"Stay here," Widow said, and walked over to it.

Amita stayed behind.

He walked over to the body and drew his gun, keeping it down by his side, pointed at the ground. It was cold in his hand, but somehow it felt like it belonged there, like he had been born with a gun in hand.

Widow stopped at the corpse and looked around. The flames in the remnants of the house bounced in the air, allowing him to see for about a hundred yards in a 360-degree radius. Orange and red hues flashed on the bottoms of the branches of the nearby trees like strange reflections. The heat had melted the snow from the branches and the foundation of the house.

The only thing not burning on the house was the brick steps that had once led to the front door and probably to a porch. Widow imagined a big front porch. He imagined that when Jacobs was a boy, he and his father had built the porch together. They had hammered nails into the wood and shingled the roof and painted the whole thing. Maybe they had even hung a porch swing. A father and son working together, bonding. Something he had never experienced. And then years later, Mr. Gareth had come along and enjoyed the fruits of their labor. And now he was dead.

Widow studied the surrounding area. There was no one around. No bad guys. No more bodies. He looked down and investigated the dead body in front of him. It was completely charred. Nothing left but a dark, shriveled shell of a man. No way to identify him. Anything that had been in his pockets was burned to ash. His face was scorched to the bone. He had died a horrible, agonizing death. No question.

The only way to make a positive identification of the dead guy would be by teeth or fingerprints. The guy had worn gloves. Perhaps some of his fingerprints would still be intact. Widow examined him more closely. Most of his clothes were burned to a crisp. No way to tell anything about him from those, but he was well-armed—strapped to his leg was a half-charred gun. Widow grabbed it and pulled it out of the hip holster. The holster came apart, and some of it still stuck to the gun, fused by the heat of the flames. The gun was still warm, but not hot. It looked like a Beretta, a badly damaged one. No way to be sure, but it was most likely a nine millimeter.

There was also an all-steel three-inch knife shoved into a sheath on the guy's belt. Most of the belt had been scorched to nothing, just like the rest of him. But the knife was still intact. It was still a little warm from the fire. Widow pulled it out. Good knife. No reason to waste it. He couldn't keep it. He had nowhere to store it. It didn't fold up, but he could put it to good use.

This body might be Jacobs, but there was no way to identify his body by sight. Widow grabbed the guy's hand and peeled one finger free from the gloves. On inspection, it looked like the fingerprint was still visible on his left-hand index finger.

Widow hacked off the finger with one hard stab from the knife. The blade plunged deep into the ground beneath the hand. It breached the snow, burying the blade up to the hilt in sleet. The tip of the finger popped off. He left the knife where it was and scooped up the fingertip. He had nothing to wrap it up in, so he just slipped it into his coat pocket—opposite side from the P99.

He returned to Amita.

She said, "Who is it? Is it him?"

"I don't know who it is."

"Should I look?" she asked.

"No. No point. Not even his mother would recognize him now."

Amita asked, "What are we going to do?"

Widow said, "The power is on at the station house, right?"

"Generator."

"I took his fingerprint," Widow said.

Amita asked, "How? You have a fingerprint kit?"

"I mean, I *took* his fingerprint."

Amita asked before she realized what he meant. He had taken his finger. She said, "We can send it to the FBI. See who he is."

Widow stayed quiet.

"What do you think happened here?"

Widow said, "I don't know for sure."

He walked away from her and stood over some shrapnel from the explosion. The front yard was littered with tiny fragments of the house. Some of the larger pieces far from the house still burned. No sign of Jacobs, unless the dead guy was him.

Widow walked around some more. They stared at something about fifty feet from the south side of the house.

There were large, deep imprints in the snow that probably reached into the soil below. Widow wasn't sure what they were. The imprints were in the shape of a triangle. Each was several feet apart. There were no other tracks.

He peered up at the sky. There was a clearing above the area and the house. Just open air.

Amita asked, "What?"

Widow stayed quiet.

"Widow, what is it?"

Widow walked back to the charred corpse and studied it closer. Then he walked back to the fire and stared at it. Widow circled the house and searched the perimeter thoroughly. He returned to the corpse and searched farther away from it. He made it all the way to the trees before he saw a black object buried in the snow. Lone and black. The deadly end pointed directly at him. The safer end was buried deep in the snow. He reached down and grabbed it. It was an ultrashort assault rifle by Heckler and Koch—the G36C. It had a collapsible stock, and a silencer attached. No scope. The G36C fired a 5.56-millimeter NATO round. It wasn't as powerful as a rocket launcher, but it was far from a pellet gun. This was a serious weapon. Expensive and more likely used by mercenaries.

The G36C had been buried to the trigger in the snow. It was backward, so Widow figured that there was probably no snow packed into the muzzle. Even if there had been, chances were that he could remove the silencer, and the muzzle would still be clear of snow. He figured it would fire just fine. Just to be safe. Widow unscrewed the silencer, slipped it into his coat pocket. He ejected the magazine and cocked the gun, and a live round popped out of the side door. He repeated the action, and nothing happened. There were no more rounds in the gun. He inspected the muzzle and looked into the barrel. There was no trace of snow. He reinserted the magazine and aimed it up into the trees and set the gun to single round fire. Then he breathed in and squeezed the trigger. The gun fired—loud. The sound echoed through the trees and across the landscape and died off in the clouds. The gun worked just fine.

He brushed the remaining snow from around the stock and the handle. There was no strap, so he set the safety and held the gun one-handed with the muzzle pointed downward and his palm around the magazine.

He turned and walked back around the house one more time. This time, he walked back to the triangles in the snow and then saw something behind them. He walked a little farther and saw a pile of large, shiny metal objects. It looked like someone had dumped a large box full of coins onto the ground. After a moment studying the metal objects, he grabbed one and squeezed it in his palm. He walked back over to Amita, who was standing by the horses, holding their reins in one hand.

She pointed at the assault rifle under his arm and asked, "What the hell is that?"

"It's a Heckler and Koch G36C. Slightly modified."

"Modified?"

"Silencer," he said. He pulled it out of his pocket, showed it to her, and slipped it back into his pocket.

She asked, "Where the hell did you get it?"

"I'm assuming the charred body brought it with him."

She asked, "Is it Mike? Do you think?"

"I don't. I think that the dead guy over there was trying to attack the house. Mr. Gareth here was a casualty. Jacobs was probably holed up inside, and he and Mr. Gareth tried to defend the house from invaders."

Amita said, "Invaders?"

Widow said, "Yeah. Looks like a siege."

"A siege?"

"Right."

"So… what? Mike came to his old home to hide out, and Mr. Gareth let him stay. Then the terrorist attacked the house, and it exploded?"

"Could be."

"Is Mike dead inside? Or you think they got him?"

Widow said, "I don't know. But I doubt these were the terrorists. At least they aren't Native American ones. That's what they told me I was up against here."

"So, what then?"

"Best guess?"

Amita said, "Yes."

"Two things. First, they're well financed."

"And?"

"And desperate. I think there's something valuable at play here, and these terrorists, whoever they are, are desperate to get Jacobs."

"How do you know the terrorists are Native Americans?"

"That's what they told me."

"But the CIA isn't exactly famous for telling the truth."

Widow nodded and said, "That's true. There's more. They also told me this wild story about a canister of weaponized Ebola."

Amita's jaw dropped, and she said, "What the hell? You didn't think to tell us this earlier?"

"Honestly, I didn't believe it. Not then."

"Why not?"

Widow said, "Weaponized Ebola? On a Native American reservation? It sounds more like fiction. It's hard enough for me to swallow a story about a terrorist cell made up of local Native Americans and a missing undercover CIA agent."

"So, do you think these CIA guys are lying to you?"

"One."

"What?"

"I only met with one CIA guy: Shepard. He told me the whole story. I thought he was full of shit. But now…"

"Now what?"

"Now, I'm not so sure."

"Why?"

Widow said, "I doubted the story about the Native American terrorists. But there are definitely bad guys here, and they're the serious type. A Heckler and Koch G36 is expensive equipment. Plus…"

"Plus, what?"

"Look around. Look at the ground. It's covered in snow."

"Yeah?"

"Besides the dog tracks leading from the house, what other tracks do you see?"

Amita looked at the ground. She ignored the shrapnel and studied the snow. She said, "Footprints. Lots of them."

"What else?"

She looked again, and then she said, "Nothing. Nothing else."

"So how did these guys get here?"

Amita said nothing.

Widow said, "We had to ride horseback up the mountain. This house was attacked by several guys. There are footprints everywhere—and different sets. Right?"

She nodded.

"By my count, there were at least five guys—five sets of foreign footprints. One is dead. I doubt they walked up the mountain. How did they get here?"

Amita nodded. "How?"

"Think about the boy. He said he heard a loud engine."

"A snowcat?"

"Where are the tracks?"

Amita said nothing.

Widow shook his head. He pointed at the triangle where the deep holes were. He said, "Helicopter. The bad guys have a helicopter. Those are landing gear marks. The helicopter has retractable wheels."

Amita stared at the holes in the ground.

"And how did the house explode exactly?" Widow asked.

Amita shook her head.

Widow opened his hand and revealed the metal object he had found in the snow. It was a shell casing for M50 ammunition. It was a colossal bullet casing. Huge. The bullet would rip a limb off. It would tear a hole through a man so fast it would knock him off his feet before the bullet exited. It could shoot through an engine block. No problem.

"They blew the house up with machine gun rounds from a big gun."

Amita's face turned as white as a ghost.

Widow said, "There's a mountain of these casings over there by the landing gear marks. I think this was from a Vulcan machine gun, which is a turret attached to a helicopter. Normally, a military helicopter would have this kind of weapon. That means our terrorists aren't only well financed; they're also well equipped. I didn't believe they were after Ebola. Not at first. But now, I'd believe anything. They went through a lot of trouble here. Maybe they aren't Native American, but they are after something valuable. A weaponized disease is as good a thing to be after as anything else."

Amita said, "What next?"

Widow said, "Next, we go back to the station. The storm will be back soon. We need to send off the fingerprint. Find out who this guy is. I need to call Shepard."

32

THEY RODE the horses all the way back to the police station. There was no reason to return them to the ranch. They locked them up in a large, heated shed behind the community center. The situation required immediacy, and Amita figured she could apologize to the rancher later.

They reached the station just in the nick of time because not five minutes later; the winds picked up, and the snow hammered them again. It was slow at first, but it sped up steadily and would be blinding within an hour.

Widow called Shepard. He stayed outside the station house while Amita went in. He pulled out the sat phone Shepard had given him and opened it up, clicked it on. The light at the top blinked a blue color, and the screen lit up. He looked at the contacts. There was only one—Shepard. He dialed it.

There was a hum and a whine as the phone was relayed through satellites miles above the earth. Then there was a dial tone and a ring. Widow waited. A voice came on.

"Widow?"

"It's me."

Shepard said, "What's the status? Did you find him?"

Widow said, "No. Not sure he's alive. But something is going on here."

"What do you mean?"

Widow thought for a second. He wasn't sure he could trust Shepard. Certainly, the man was hiding things from him. That was what he did for a living—he lied to people and kept secrets.

"There was an attack on the reservation. House explosion. It looked like a siege. Dead bodies. Evidence of a helicopter."

The line was silent.

Widow said, "Is there something you're not telling me?"

"I told you everything that pertains to the situation."

"You're sticking to the story of Ebola?"

"That part is real. It's imperative that you locate Jacobs."

Widow stayed quiet.

Shepard asked, "Is he dead? If he is, did you get a visual confirmation?"

Widow said, "No. No body."

"The clock is ticking. The CIA will not allow the weapon to be removed from the reservation."

"What does that mean?" Widow asked.

"You know what it means. You've got the same time limit as before. Unless you have good news for me by the time the storm subsides, I'll be forced to notify the Air Force of a new domestic target for them to bomb."

Widow stayed quiet.

The whole story and threat seemed unbelievable to him—almost. But he knew from his own experience that governmental cover-up was a real thing. A guy like Shepard didn't strike him as the type of guy who bluffed, not with national security. And things were far beyond believability already. The bad guys had a helicopter with guns on it. The nearest government with military helicopters that would loan them out to terrorists against America was probably an ocean away. Canada wouldn't do it in a thousand years, and Mexico's military probably couldn't afford a helicopter like that. Therefore, the craft was stolen and belonged to a group with access to foreign military arms, or it was a civilian helicopter, heavily modified aftermarket.

None of these options made Widow feel any better.

He said, "Shepard, you need to do some research to find out who might have access to a military helicopter. It must be stationed nearby. Probably parked on a rooftop or a clearing within a hundred miles. No way would they get far in this weather."

Shepard said, "I'll do that. If it isn't a local band of ragtag terrorists, then we've got bigger problems, which means we'll have no option other than erasing the reservation. We can't let the Ebola canister get outside of that area."

Widow gripped the phone tightly, but said nothing.

"Get on it. Call me ASAP," Shepard said and hung up the phone.

33

ONE LESSON military life had taught him was to *sleep when you can*. It was imperative to sleep when he could because, in the field, he never knew when he'd get the next opportunity. Better to be rested than the alternative. More mistakes were made in the field due to fatigue than any other reason.

Widow did two things after talking to Shepard on the sat phone.

The first was to get the fingerprint from the severed finger he had carried back with him. Amita refused to touch it, so he inked it and fingerprinted it. Amita took the sheet with the dead guy's fingerprint and faxed it to the FBI while the phone lines were still up. Widow watched her do it, and then he told her she had better try to get some sleep. He said he'd do the same.

The second thing he did was check on the Mexican boy. The kid was already fast asleep.

Widow returned to the police station and parked himself in the cell that he'd already slept one night in. It was starting to feel like a second home. He took off his coat and left it hanging on the back of a chair that had been pulled into the cell from the bullpen. He left the G36 leaning up against the inside wall. Then he dumped himself down on the bed, lay down fully clothed, and shut his eyes—time to sleep.

Sleep when you can.

34

THE SNOWSTORM THUNDERED and roared every so often in spaced-out intervals, alerting Widow's ears. But he slept fine. The sounds would stir him for a moment, and then he'd drift back to sleep—no big deal. Nothing lost. Widow had slept through snowstorms before and was familiar with the noises that accompanied them.

Amita stood out in front of the community center, talking to her father. She explained to him everything that was going on and filled him in on the things he didn't know. The dead bodies. The fire. Ebola. Everything.

Red Cloud stroked his face, feeling the stubble from not shaving for a day underneath his fingers. A look of great worry fell across his face, a look she hadn't seen in years. The last time she had seen it was the day she told him she wanted to run away with Mike Jacobs.

Red Cloud said, "What do you make of the boy? What does he have to do with this mess?"

Amita ignored the question and asked, "Has he said anything else?"

"Not in English. He only seems to speak Spanish. Which I guess makes sense because that boy is Mexican. No doubt about it. He's a long way from home."

Amita said, "I don't know what he's doing here. Widow doesn't either. You know…"

"What?"

"Nothing."

"Amita, tell me."

"Widow's a pretty smart guy. Why does he live like a bum?"

Red Cloud said, "He's not. Technically."

"He's homeless."

Red Cloud said, "True, but he migrates from place to place. So technically, he isn't a bum. He's a drifter, a hobo."

"Why does he do that? Why live that way? He's a smart guy. He could be doing something with his life."

"I agree, but it's his life. Maybe he knows something we don't."

* * *

THE SMALL BOY rolled over on his cot and opened his eyes. He had forgotten where he was for a moment and felt scared. Then he remembered his friend had rescued him. He remembered his friend was still out there and would come for him. He believed that.

He thought about the monster man. The monster man had been nice to him, too. Like his amigo, the one who saved him. The boy wondered if they were friends, the monster man and his amigo. The boy wondered if the monster man was here to protect him, too. He sat upright and turned his head to look right. Then he looked left. He saw no one he knew. There were a lot of old people here. They were all asleep.

The boy listened to the wind howl and moan. He looked down the aisle for the monster man, but saw no sign of him. The boy felt scared because he wasn't nearby, so he slipped off the bed to look for him. His feet were bare, and he felt the floor was cold underneath his toes. He knew that feeling. He had cement floors at his parents' house, down in Mexico.

The kid walked quietly away from the cot, and then he stopped and went back. He had forgotten his toy. He picked up the little black device and watched the light blink. Then he moved again and walked down the aisles between the people. He looked at every face, but there was no sign of the monster man.

The small boy went down the hall and turned into a large room he thought looked like a police station, like from his favorite TV shows. He walked past a desk and through a doorway. He had seen a doorway like that before. It was the type of doorway that detected metal. It stayed silent as he went through it. He walked around some more desks, checking between them and under them—still no sign of the monster man.

He heard a rumbling noise and turned. There were rooms with bars in front of them. He walked over to the first one and peered in. There was no one there. He moved to the second one and looked in. And then he saw him, the monster man. He was sprawled out on a thin bed.

The boy giggled at this because the monster man was far too big to be sleeping on such a thin bed. He looked funny.

The boy walked closer and pulled out his device. The light was blinking faster, but he didn't know why. He reached up and tugged on the monster man's sleeve.

35

THE NIGHT PASSED and grew old—either that or the morning was young. If days were measured in a life cycle, then this day was an old, dying man or a young kid, depending on when the birth cycle started. So if midnight was death, and zero hour was birth, then this day was young.

The snowstorm bellowed and boomed every so often, alerting Widow's ears. But he stayed asleep with no problems. The sounds would grow and diminish and then return. After several hours of this, they lessened and finally stopped.

Widow would've slept until the morning except that he felt something tugging at him. So he opened his eyes abruptly, startled. He realized something was pulling at his sleeve. He craned his neck without sitting up and looked directly into the eyes of the Mexican boy.

"Hey, kid," he said.

The boy replied something in Spanish. It was too fast for Widow to translate—his Spanish wasn't fluent, but low—intermediate. High school foreign language only got a man so far. Widow sat up. The Mexican boy repeated what he was saying. Despite that, Widow didn't understand him, so he merely nodded.

The boy reached his hand out, palm up, and showed something to him. It was a small black device with twinkling light on it. Widow snatched it up and studied it. The boy didn't seem to mind.

Widow said, "Shit!"

36

THE DEVICE WAS A TRACKER, something that looked like it'd be used by Special Forces. Widow studied it. He saw no trademarks. No logos. No "Made in China" label. No English writing or any other language. Nothing that'd help him discern its origin.

Widow figured it was definitely some kind of covert ops equipment.

He looked at the boy and asked, "Where did you get this?"

The boy shrugged.

Widow said, "¿De dónde surgió desde?" But he wasn't one hundred percent certain he was saying the right thing.

The boy said something else in Spanish, and Widow didn't follow. Then the boy said, "Bad guy. Copper."

Widow knew he was talking about a bad guy from the helicopter. He got up out of bed.

The little boy looked up at him with confused brown eyes.

Widow held out his hand gently, and the little boy grabbed it. He led the boy back through the police station, down the hall, and into the community center. They crept through, trying not to wake anyone. Widow peered around, studying faces, looking for Amita and her father. He heard voices in the distance.

He went outside and found them standing near the entrance. The freezing weather engulfed his face.

The boy had followed close behind him. He nudged him back inside and said, "Wait."

Widow went back out into the cold.

Amita said, "You're awake. Neither of us could sleep. Not that we should, anyway. Not with all that's going on."

Widow studied her face. She looked tired. Dark circles nestled under her eyes, and her makeup was practically gone at this point. Her father looked even worse. He needed sleep. His face was worn like old leather. He looked more like a great grandfather than a fifty-five-year-old father.

Widow said, "You two should've gotten some sleep."

Amita said, "We'll sleep tomorrow."

It reminded Widow of a guy he used to serve with years ago. Another SEAL who always said, "I'll sleep tomorrow." Which was a spin on the phrase "I'll sleep when I'm dead," another common Navy SEAL motto. However, the guy who used to say that; died on a mission.

Widow always slept when he could.

He asked, "Do you see this?" He showed them the device. "I found the boy with it."

The father said, "I saw him with it earlier. What is it?"

"It's a tracker. He must've gotten it off one of the bad guys, probably the dead one. The charred guy. I think he picked it up while he was escaping. Then he collapsed in the cold, and the dead dog we found dragged him through the snow and down the mountain until it died from the gunshot wound. The bad guys must've been shooting at him."

Amita asked, "Why would they shoot at a little boy?"

"I don't think they were trying to kill him. I think maybe they were trying to recover him."

"Why?"

"I don't know. But there's a lot more going on here than a canister of Ebola."

"What else is going on?"

Widow said, "Something to do with this boy. He's from Mexico—we can safely assume that—but how did he get here?"

Red Cloud asked, "Where are his parents?"

Amita shrugged.

"We need to find Jacobs," Widow said. "He holds the answers."

Amita asked, "Is he alive?"

"We haven't found him dead. Maybe he was in the fire, but maybe not. If he didn't die, and the bad guys didn't get what they wanted, then they'll be back. The boy picked up this tracker, not knowing what it was. It's used by special forces teams to keep track of their guys. It's usually sewn into their equipment—like a rucksack—for keeping tabs on them.

"The kid picked it up. It's not meant to track him, so they may not be looking at it. But they might, and that means they know where he is. Or they will—soon."

Widow found a patch on concrete, kicked off the snow, dropped the tracker and stomped on it hard. Once. Twice. Three times. It shattered into tiny fragments. He kicked them off into the snow.

He said, "We'd better get ready. This storm is slowing down. We may have visitors. Amita, you'd better check to see if the FBI responded on that print. We need to know who we're dealing with. And call them. And call the state police. We'll need some backup."

"What about the CIA?"

"They aren't going to help us. But I'll call Shepard, anyway. Can't hurt to ask."

Widow pulled out the sat phone and dialed and let it ring and ring.

Shepard answered, "Widow, have you found him yet?"

"I don't know where the hell you got your intel from, but it's a joke."

"What the hell are you talking about?"

"We got some problems up here. But I can tell you that there's no Native American terrorist group. There's a much bigger threat here."

"What?"

"There's an outside hostile force."

Shepard said, "What are you talking about?"

"If you want to get the canister of Ebola back, then you need to quarantine the reservation and send in the National Guard. We've got a well-armed force coming up here from out there."

"What?" Shepard asked again.

"Someone attacked Jacobs at a nearby house and blew it up. And, Shepard, they've got some impressive firearms. I found a Heckler and Koch G36."

Silence on the other end of the line.

Widow said, "And better than that, they've also got a military chopper. Loaded with a machine gun."

"Military chopper? You sure?"

"About as sure as I can be. I saw the tracks from the landing gear. And they used a Vulcan machine gun to destroy a house."

Shepard repeated, "You sure?"

"Yes, I'm sure. There were shell casings from the bullets all over the ground."

Silence again.

Shepard said, "This is serious. We'll get you out of there. You're right—this situation is too big for us. We'll have to involve the governor and the National Guard. Just stay put for now. I'll get back to you."

Then Shepard clicked off, and the line went dead.

Widow stared at the phone and slipped it into his pocket. Amita had walked away while he was on the call. He looked at the chief.

Red Cloud said, "This Shepard doesn't seem trustworthy."

"The CIA never is."

"What do you think?"

Widow said, "I don't know yet. But we can't wait. We need to find Jacobs. He'll know something."

Amita came back out of the community center, holding a fax in her hand. She showed it to them. Half of the page was blank, like it had gotten cut off in the transmission.

Red Cloud said, "I'm going to head back in. I left my radio inside, charging."

Widow nodded, and they watched him walk back.

Amita turned back to Widow and said, "The phone lines went down right in the middle of receiving. The internet is out too. Right now, your sat phone is the only working communicator."

"And that'll only last as long as the weather holds up," Widow said.

"You have to see what the FBI sent about this guy. There's something seriously wrong with it."

Widow looked at it. The guy's name was Cory Philips. There was all the basic background Widow had expected— a place of birth, age, college, military service, Special Forces training, tours in Iraq, redacted missions, and so on.

The one thing that was unusual was that Cory Philips had died two years ago in a helicopter crash.

37

THE SNOW CONTINUED TO FALL, but it was no longer a flurry. The clouds were spreading apart, and the skies were clearing. Widow knew this meant that Shepard would get eager for news on Jacobs. So far, all they had was no terrorist cell, no Jacobs, and no sign of a weaponized Ebola. Instead, they had a dead mercenary, who was apparently supposed to have been dead years ago, and an unknown Mexican boy.

Widow asked, "What the hell is going on?"

"I don't know, but I think your CIA agent is lying to you," Amita said.

"I know he's lying. But what about?"

"What do you think?"

Widow said, "I think he's telling the truth about Jacobs. And he might be telling us the truth about the terrorists. Someone is definitely attacking us. But I'm not sure about the Ebola thing."

"Maybe his ass is on the line for something else. Maybe he's just using you because you aren't affiliated with them. Plausible deniability," Amita said.

"Makes sense."

"Call him back and ask him. Confront him."

Widow said, "No. Better if we find Jacobs ourselves. Get the truth."

Just then, Amita's radio burst to life. The radio waves were working again. The storm had ceased enough to allow for the antennas to receive transmissions. Amita's father had returned to the station house after the last call with Shepard and was now on the channel. He wanted to check the radio.

He said, "Amita. You guys come inside."

Amita acknowledged with an affirmative, and they headed back inside.

They reached the double doors and found Red Cloud waiting for them just inside the entrance. He said, "Ray Collins, who lives up there on the mountain, just came down. He's in back, and he's scared. He's spouting off something about an intruder in his house."

Widow said, "Where does he live exactly?"

"He's the closest neighbor to Jacobs's house," Amita said.

"We'd better talk to him."

They went into the community center, following Red Cloud. Inside, the people were fully awake or waking up. They sat on the floor or on cots side by side. There were folding chairs along the back walls with people sitting and facing each other, deep in conversation.

Red Cloud said, "He's over there."

He pointed to a short, bald man with a long dark-blue sweater and thick boots caked in snow. Widow figured he must've run from his house and marched straight to the community center.

Amita walked over to him first, greeted him, and patted his shoulders. She had a genuine concern in her eyes. Widow thought she would make a fine police chief someday.

She had brought him a coffee and a blanket, and spent some time talking with him and not asking questions and not interrogating him. Just making him feel comfortable—safe.

Amita asked Collins to explain what was going on now that he was calmer.

Widow figured he must have frantically burst in on the large group of sleeping people, waking everyone up, probably startling them. And that's why everyone was awake.

Widow could see on their faces that they were all confused and scared.

Ray Collins still had some fear left in his voice. He described a scene where a colossal explosion woke him. The Jacobses' house, Widow presumed. About twenty minutes after that, a man with a gun barged into his house. He didn't recognize the guy. He said the guy's face was covered in blood and snow and grime. But he said it was strange because the intruder knew his name.

The guy made him wait for a while. Then he took the keys to his truck, even though it couldn't be driven because of the snow. And finally, the guy just let him go. He told him to run and not come back for a few days.

Amita didn't wait for any more of the story. She pulled Widow by the arm and said into his ear, "We'd better get up there. Must be one of the bad guys."

Widow shook his head and said, "I doubt it. Why would he let Mr. Collins go?"

Amita stayed quiet.

Widow said, "I think we've found Jacobs."

38

BEFORE THEY LEFT, Widow decided it was best to take the Heckler and Koch G36 with him. First, he took it outside and test-fired it, like he had the P99. It worked perfectly. With single-shot fire selected, he aimed and fired a round straight through the same fence, the same target. He hit almost the same area.

Amita shook her head and acted unimpressed.

Widow needed a strap to carry the gun, so he asked if Amita had anything like an old pair of boots. He could use the laces. She took him into the station house and opened a cabinet of what appeared to be lost-and-found items. Widow found a pair of boots and looked at the size. They were one inch bigger than his, which was acceptable. So instead of taking the laces from the boots, he took off his own shoes and traded them for the boots. After he'd laced them up and tested them and was satisfied, he grabbed one of the old shoes and took the shoelace out. He tied one end of the lace to the handle of the gun, made a tight knot, and then tied a duplicate knot to the stock. Now he had a usable strap. He double-checked that the safety was on and slung the gun over his shoulder and across his back, carrying it like an ancient barbarian might carry a sword.

Widow asked, "Do you have a long gun available?"

Amita said, "I have a shotgun in my police cruiser."

"Get it."

He then unlaced the other shoelace and readied it. He waited. One minute. Two. Then Amita returned with the shotgun. It had no strap either, as Widow had figured. So he tied two more knots, duplicating the same results for Amita. One knot around the barrel and one around the stock. Amita slung it across her back. And now they were a pair of ancient warriors, prepared to fight their way across the land on horseback.

Widow smiled.

AMITA AND WIDOW mounted the horses and headed out onto the snowy terrain and up the mountain. They followed a similar route as before, making a similar journey, and using the same amount of time, only they turned at a junction that Widow hadn't paid attention to the last time and veered off to the northeast. They came to a clearing and an open spot of land that must have been a snow-covered driveway. There was a timeworn wooden house standing tall with large windows that were much newer than the rest of the structure. Hurricane windows, Widow guessed. There was a flagpole with no flag. It was surrounded by a small stone base. The rope on the pole flapped and batted up against the steel.

Widow saw that the snow had covered the steps leading up to the house, but there were footprints through it. And there was clearly a path of footprints that led off toward the main center of the reservation.

"Mr. Collins," Amita said, looking at the footprints.

Widow nodded. He imagined Collins being confronted by CIA agent Mike Jacobs. Jacobs took him hostage, but only to keep him safe from the bad guys in case there were more of them. Then, when the coast was clear, Jacobs let him go and probably buckled down for the rest of the night to ride out the storm. Since Collins was still alive and had only just arrived at the community center, then he probably left his house a little over an hour ago. Running down the mountain—gravity on his side and adrenaline pumping through his veins, not to mention the fear driving him—the guy probably made impressive time. Maybe even less than an hour. Widow hoped Jacobs was still there.

They made their way into the clearing and approached. Not wanting to close in on horseback in case the intruder started shooting at them, they tied the horses off on the mailbox at the end of the drive. Better to approach on foot.

They both drew their long guns and readied them—the shotgun in Amita's hand and the G36 in Widow's. Widow took point. He led Amita up to the house. The occupants would've probably heard the horses in the distance, but maybe not. So far, they had no problems.

The goal of approaching a house with armed combatants inside was to reach cover quickly and quietly. Widow had no problem with the quiet part, but moving fast in the snow wasn't easy. He had to watch where he stepped while watching the house for signs of the enemy. Amita approached from the left, and Widow came in from the right. He glanced at every window and back to the front door—no sign of awareness by the hostile inside. Amita was faster and quieter than Widow because she was much lighter. She crept up and reached the porch before he did. She stopped, turned, and kept the shotgun pointed at the front door.

Widow made it up onto the porch. The boards creaked underneath his bulk, and he paused a beat to wait to see if anyone had heard him. Nothing happened. So he continued over to Amita, and they paused in front of the door.

She leaned into him and whispered, "I should announce 'police.'"

Widow whispered back, "Don't do it. Let's breach."

She nodded.

They prepared to breach the entrance. Amita stood back to the left of the door, and Widow stood in front, in a position to kick the door in. First, he reached forward and tried the knob slowly, prepared to jump right in case gunfire came back at him from the other side of the door. The knob turned, and the door popped open with a faint groan. Widow moved to the right with his G36 pointed at the entrance. He pushed the door open with the muzzle. The door swung ajar, and Widow peeked in. He saw nothing.

He opened it all the way and stepped in, sweeping his gun slowly from side to side, checking corners and doorways. No movement. Nothing happened.

The house was mostly dark. A dim light from a lamp lit up the living room and shone on the floor in the hallway. There were pictures of kids and grandkids littering the walls. Widow saw bloody handprints smeared down the wall toward the stairs. One print was right on top of a picture of the whole Collins family.

Amita followed Widow with the shotgun pointed in the opposite direction and downward. She was careful to keep him out of the area of fire. He gestured to her to show her the prints along the wall. She looked at them and nodded. Together, they thought of the possibility that the intruder was wounded. They continued to search the hallway and found nothing.

The living room had more family pictures. The owner apparently had no television. Widow liked that. It was obvious what the old guy did for entertainment, because, on the eastern wall, there was a huge bookshelf. It stretched the length of the wall—about ten feet. Widow took a glance at the books and scanned the titles. Lots of science fiction. Old titles too.

Then they heard a noise from above—a *creak* and a *thud*. They turned and headed quickly to the staircase. It was in the hallway and faced an open doorway, which led to the kitchen. The kitchen was wide open. They could see into it without having to enter. There were no hiding places. They both pointed their guns up the stairs and waited.

No movement.

A light stretched out across the top landing and over the top three steps.

Widow took point again. He placed his hand up in the air and closed his fist—standard military signal to stop. He hoped she'd understand. And she did, because she halted. He went first.

The G36 was smooth and comfortable in his hands, an extension of himself. One thought, and his finger would squeeze the trigger and kill the first hostile he saw. But no one came out at him. No one moved from the top floor. As he neared the top, he saw that there was only one room. It was an open bedroom. And it was huge. It took up the entire top floor.

Widow topped the stairs and entered the bedroom. More books here. They were stacked up high—three feet in some places. The bed was king-sized, and Widow was sure Mr. Collins felt lonely if he slept in it alone. There were no signs of a female inhabitant. Widow figured Mr. Collins had lost his wife. He imagined the old guy lived alone—a widower who never remarried.

A lonely life, Widow thought—solitary like his own. He understood the attraction to such a life. Some people were meant to be settled down. Some people were comfortable with that. But others were not. Apparently, Mr. Collins had tried it both ways.

Widow lowered the gun because lying on the bed and snoring like a man who hadn't slept in days was the lone intruder. The noise they'd heard must've been him collapsing in exhaustion.

Amita looked and said, "That's Mike."

He was covered in blood, but obviously alive and well.

39

Blood covered CIA agent Mike Jacobs's clothes, but apparently, none of it was his because there were no visible wounds on the man. In addition, he snored like a man in a serious coma, and Widow had never heard a man who was bleeding to death sleeping so soundly.

Amita set down her shotgun and went over to Jacobs like a woman still in love. She had recognized his face. Widow imagined that the only difference was that this guy was probably a lot thinner than he once was. Widow figured he had been heavier at one time because his body was bony and frail. It looked like he hadn't eaten in weeks. There were two open and empty boxes of cereal on the bed, as well as two empty bottles of mineral water.

Widow guessed he had fought the mercenaries at the family house and killed one, getting the guy's blood all over him, and then ran here. He hadn't eaten or slept for days. Perhaps he had been holed up somewhere in his old house. Maybe in the attic. Maybe the old guy who lived there, Mr. Gareth, hadn't even known he was there, and Jacobs's stowing away in his attic got the guy killed. Widow figured that was why he had sent Collins out on his own so quickly—to keep another innocent man from being killed because of his actions.

Amita shook Jacobs and said, "Mike? Mike? Wake up!"

Widow stayed quiet. He looked down at a Beretta nine millimeter that lay on the bed. He picked it up. It was light. He ejected the magazine. The gun was empty. He pulled back the slider. No bullet chambered.

Widow said, "He fired all of his bullets back at the Garret house. He took Collins hostage, with no intention of hurting him. And I think it's obvious that this has something to do with the Mexican boy."

Amita stopped shaking him, turned, and said, "Of course."

Widow stared next to the bed at something out of her view.

She asked, "What?"

Widow said, "I bet this case will tell us something." He reached down and picked up a bulletproof briefcase, showed it to her.

She stared at it, confused, and she asked, "Is that the Ebola?"

Widow said, "No way! It wouldn't be in a briefcase."

"It looks tough," Amita said.

"It's bulletproof, no doubt about that, but it's not made to transport a biological weapon. It'd have to be a lot bigger, and it would be a different metal."

"So, what's inside?"

Widow plopped it down on the bed near Jacobs and looked at the combination lock on the outer lip. He said, "Find a toolbox. We need a hammer."

Amita nodded and got up and headed downstairs. She went straight to the kitchen and checked under the sink, which she figured was the most obvious place to keep a toolbox besides a garage or a toolshed.

She found a large toolbox, but didn't bother opening it. She figured it was better to bring the whole thing upstairs. It was heavy. The tools inside shuffled around and rattled as she lifted it, climbed the steps, and made her way back to the bedroom. Widow got up and grabbed the toolbox one-handed. He set it down on the floor and moved the brief-case next to it—better to hammer the lock on a harder surface.

He popped open the toolbox and saw a hammer, grabbed it, slid the toolbox aside, and then hammered hard at the combination lock. It took three blows, and the lock was destroyed. Widow flipped the hammer and pried open the case with the hammer's claw. After two powerful attempts, the case popped open. Widow jerked up on both feet like a jack-in-the-box. Amita covered her mouth, which had dropped open in shock.

They both stared without blinking for almost a minute. Soundless and silent. Nothing could be heard in the entire house except for the light snow hitting the roof and the contented snoring from Jacobs.

If the bad guys had shown up, attack helicopter and all, and started firing at the house, they might still be stuck there staring at the contents of the briefcase.

The briefcase's contents sparkled and glimmered at them. The case was full of diamonds. More diamonds than Widow imagined he'd ever see in real life.

40

"SCARED THE SHIT OUT OF ME" is a common expression. And those were the words that best expressed how Mike Jacobs felt when he woke up to see Widow standing over him.

He woke up in a strange bed in a strange house. He had confusion and fear in his eyes, and Widow watched as he reached quickly for his Beretta. But Widow had moved it, not that it would've mattered since it was empty, anyway.

Amita stepped into view and said, "Mike, calm down. It's me."

Jacobs said, "Amita?"

"Yes. It's me."

"How? Where am I?"

"You don't remember?"

He sat up. It was obvious that he suffered from a headache. He felt like someone had shot an arrow right through his head.

Jacobs was a good-looking guy. He was short, probably five eight or five nine, but although he was now scrawny, it looked like he had once been solidly built. Widow figured this guy must've taken his spycraft seriously, especially the physical side of it. He put in lots of hours in the gym, unlike Widow, who had given up his gym days after he left the SEALs.

Jacobs said, "I remember… ditching a truck that I stole back in Tower Junction. And I got a ride to the reservation. I remember sneaking into my old house with… with…" He looked around, slowly at first and then frantically. Then he looked panicked. "Tomas? Tomas?"

Widow said, "He's safe."

"What? Who?" Amita asked.

Widow said, "The boy. He's safe."

Jacobs calmed and said, "Okay. Good. Where is he?"

"He made it out. We got him. He's safe in the town. With her father."

Jacobs looked relieved and nodded.

"Why don't you tell us what the hell is going on?"

"First, who are you? Are you with them?" said Jacobs.

Widow said, "I'm no one. I'm just a guy passing through. A total stranger."

He figured it was best not to mention Shepard yet. He wasn't sure if he trusted Shepard himself.

Picking up on the same idea, Amita said, "It's true. He's not with anyone. Mike, what's going on?"

Jacobs sat up and said, "I have to get Tomas and get out of here. They know we're here."

Widow said, "Slow down. Just tell us what's going on."

"There's this guy. Two years ago, he came for me. At school. I had filled out online applications everywhere. And I was rejected everywhere. But it was the CIA that called me."

Widow slipped the G36 with the homemade strap across his back, folded his arms, and listened. Amita sat down on the bed next to Jacobs and held his hand.

Jacobs said, "This guy. Shepard. He recruited me after I interviewed and sent me to the CIA farm to learn trade-craft. After that grueling experience, I was assigned to work on his team. He insisted on me. He kept vouching for me. Like I was exceptional or something." Jacobs turned in the bed and faced a large, two-panel window behind Widow. Then he said, "This guy. He's unlike anyone you'll ever meet. He can convince you of anything."

Widow nodded, said, "I know. I met the guy."

Jacobs turned white.

"Shepard picked me up in the next town. Asked me to look for you because his guys were getting nowhere. They were searching and harassing the locals, but no one knew anything," Widow said. "You're bone thin. Like a man who's been hiding out for weeks. I've seen it before with fugitives. They hide out in the woods or some abandoned house and never eat. Shepard fed me this story that you were undercover and looking for a terrorist group on the reservation. Searching for a missing canister of Ebola."

Jacobs looked confused. Then he said, "I'm thin because of the guilt. I stopped eating a while ago. Then I ran."

Widow nodded and continued, "I never really bought into it. Not really. I believed he was CIA. I believed you were missing. He didn't want to tell me the truth, and I accepted that. But a missing weaponized biochemical weapon on a Native American reservation? It seemed ridiculous. But he was very convincing. I figured it was something."

Amita said, "When did you figure he was lying?"

Widow said, "I always knew it. But I didn't know he was the bad guy in all of this until just now. Look at how white Jacobs turned when I mentioned his name." Widow turned to Jacobs and said, "Why don't you tell us why you're so scared of him."

Jacobs said, "He's evil. Pure evil."

"What has he done?" Amita asked.

"He really is a CIA agent—that part's true. But he's twisted."

Widow said, "A lot of them are. I've had experience with them in the past."

"Shepard's in the moneymaking business and not so much the spy business," Jacobs said, paused and then said, "The man's a hero to the CIA because he has an impressive track record for acquiring information. But his methods are…" He paused again and swallowed and said, "Terrifying."

Widow stayed quiet.

Jacobs said, "He's in the ransom business. My first time out with him was two weeks ago. I was nervous and scared and excited. He picked me up at a Texas airport, and we drove to Fort Hood. They had this stealth helicopter, a Comanche RAH-70. It was awesome! We flew the helicopter across the Mexican border. Our mission was to gain intel from a Mexican diplomat. He had information about a pending military coup. At least that was what Shepard told me. I don't know what's true."

Widow said, "The Comanche RAH-70. It's real?"

Jacobs nodded and said, "It's real."

"Go on."

"The CIA uses a carrot-and-stick approach. I thought we were going to start with the carrot. Only we went right to the stick. With Shepard, there is no carrot."

Amita asked, "Carrot? Stick?"

Widow said, "Carrot is money. The CIA usually pays for information, and they pay a lot for it. Money is the motivator of motivators."

"Stick?" she asked.

"The stick is something else entirely."

She said, "Like what? Like violence?"

Widow said, "Sometimes worse."

Jacobs looked at Amita. Then he looked down like he was ashamed of the next part of the story. He said, "We planned an abduction. Shepard's guys. They'd all worked with him for years. I was the only one who was new. He dressed up the mission briefing like he was explaining it to a new group. But really it was just me, like a show. I was the only rookie. The other guys are just as evil as he is. He explained it all like a routine CIA mission. Like it was the way things were done. He explained to me it was like being a cop. They teach you the classroom stuff, and then you learn the street stuff."

Jacobs stopped, looked at Amita again. Her eyes stared into his. Widow could see there was still a lot of love between them.

Widow asked, "What happened?"

Jacobs said, "They didn't tell me what we were doing. Not completely. I swear. We kidnapped this Mexican guy's wife and son. Oh god! I really didn't know!"

Widow said, "Calm down. What happened next?"

"At first, nothing happened. Shepard made it all seem routine and fake. You know, like we had to be mean to them to make them think it was real. We had to make them believe it. The guys beat the wife. Nothing major at first. Like slaps. Not even that hard. But then things progressed. They started doing it right in front of the kid. It felt real to me. Shepard could see the uneasiness on my face. He kept reminding me it was all an act. They weren't really going to do any permanent damage. He was ransoming their lives so that the Mexican guy would share information with us. This is how he always got such significant information. He used the stick. But it got worse. Much worse.

"The Mexican guy was scared for his family. Of course. So he gave up all the information Shepard wanted. He gave him the names and dates of all kinds of secret Mexican government goings-on. But Shepard wasn't satisfied. We didn't turn the family back over. Instead, they raped and killed the wife. It was slow at first. Like they all took turns. They wanted me to take part, but I didn't. I refused. I stayed with the kid. I protected him from them, but when those monsters killed his mother, I knew it was over for him as well.

"Then I found out that Shepard wanted more than information. He had ransomed the kid for diamonds—a shitload of diamonds. He made me pick them up. Shepard promised they would trade the kid for them. So I did it. I'm the only face the Mexican guy has seen. When I returned to our meeting place, they still had the kid. So I did the only thing I could. I shot one of them and took off with the kid and the diamonds.

"We stole a car and snuck across the border. I was careful all the way. I used my training to get us away from Shepard and away from Mexico. I really didn't know what I would do with the kid, but I couldn't just leave him. Shepard would kill him. So we drove on. Occasionally I traded vehicles, trying to remain untraceable.

"And we got to the reservation over a week ago. Or... I don't know. I lost time. The winter came. I kept Tomas fed, but I couldn't eat. We found food. But my nerves kept me from eating and sleeping. Finally, I passed out, and that's when they came for us. I killed one of them, but they killed

Mr. Gareth. And I thought they had taken Tomas too. But you have him?"

"He's safe. He's with my dad," Amita reminded him.

"Jacobs, I owe you an apology because I led Shepard right to you," Widow said.

Jacobs nodded, said nothing.

Widow said, "We'll deal with it."

Jacobs asked, "How?"

Widow paused a beat, and then he said, "We'll give him the stick."

41

Darkness took its last breaths. It would relinquish its life in the coming hour. Daylight slivered over the horizon and stabbed through the snow-covered trees and through the shantytown portion of Red Rain Indian Reservation.

Thirty minutes earlier, three armed men and one pilot had boarded a Comanche RAH-70, taking off and flying low, just above the trees. The rotors hummed, and the engine vibrated as silently as a helicopter could. As the sun began ascending from its sleep, the pilot could see the rotors' circular shadow wash across the tops of the trees as they flew west.

Shepard checked his Heckler and Koch G36. It was good. They were heading to the entrance of the reservation, where they had received a steady transmission from the tracking device on the guy they had lost in the attack on Gareth's house.

Shepard had spoken to the drifter, Widow, who confirmed there had been no sign of Jacobs. He had also told him that the Mexican boy was alive and on the reservation. That was all he really cared about. Jacobs was as good as dead, no matter where he was holed up. He had probably been in the house when they blew it up, anyway. And soon, the boy would be in their hands again. He would hopefully lead them back to the diamonds, and then he could be killed and discarded like so many others that they had done this to before. Shepard figured they'd probably toss him out of the helicopter as they flew back to Fort Hood.

His little body would be nearly invisible in the Texas desert from the sky. The coyotes and local critters would take care of his remains.

No problem, Shepard thought.

Of course, they would have to kill the entire population on the reservation, at least all those who were witnesses. Before they lifted off, the pilot had made sure that the Vulcan machine gun was completely loaded, and they had standby cartridges with plenty of firepower for their purposes.

The helicopter flew and yawed, then turned, and they were over the community center in minutes. The pilot hovered the craft and saw a clear spot in what looked like a snow-covered parking lot. He twisted in his seat and yelled back at Shepard.

"I'm setting her down right there!"

Shepard nodded and looked at the two agents Widow had beaten up earlier. He said, "Lock and load, boys."

The agents were dressed in thick white winter gear, and they wore Kevlar vests. Each was armed with a G36 and a Beretta holstered as a sidearm. They jumped out of the Comanche and took a stance, all facing the doors to the community center.

Shepard signaled to one guy to cover the hole leading into the police station where the door used to be, just in case someone came charging out of the darkness. The orange door still lay on the ground where the tornado had blown it off its hinges.

His guys stood ready to enter the doors to the community center.

42

AMITA RED CLOUD grabbed her radio and called her father, but no one answered the line.

She looked at Widow and said, "What if Shepard has already moved in? We've got to get back there!"

Widow nodded and said, "I'll call Shepard."

Widow pulled out the sat phone again and called Shepard.

The phone rang and rang for a long minute. Then finally, quiet breathing came over the receiver, and a voice answered in a whisper.

"Widow?" Shepard said.

"Yes. I have him."

"Who?"

Widow said, "Your man. Jacobs. And I found the case you're looking for."

Shepard paused. He signaled at his men to halt their assault on the community center.

"You've got the case?"

"I have the case and Jacobs."

"Is he alive?"

Widow said, "He is. And your diamonds are here waiting for you."

"What are you doing?" Amita whispered.

Silence fell over the line, and then Shepard said, "So then you know the truth?"

Widow said, "I do. I know you are a murderous piece of shit."

More silence.

"Be careful, son. I've got bigger guns than you."

"Where are you?" Widow asked.

Shepard said, "I'm in the middle of an interesting operation."

"The community center?"

Shepard paused, then asked, "How'd you know that?" He looked around the parking lot of the community center, thinking maybe Widow was watching him this very second.

"Because of the tracking device, I found. We figured you would come."

"You found it? What about the boy?"

Widow said, "He's here with me. We're all here. Everyone who matters, so come and get us. We'll give you what you want. No one needs to die. We just want to be rid of you."

Shepard said, "If I don't get my diamonds, you'll all die!"

Silence came over the line.

Widow said, "Tell me something. How did you get that scar across your face?"

"A lucky African hit me with a machete. It was dull. Got stuck in my face. Lucky me. But the African wasn't so lucky. He's dead… along with his family. Don't mess with me, or you'll get the same."

Widow stayed quiet.

Then Shepard said, "I come there, and you'll give me the diamonds and the boy?"

"I'll give you the diamonds. You don't need the boy or Jacobs. They're free from you now. Come get the diamonds and then go."

After a long minute, Shepard said, "You got a deal, Widow. But if you try to screw me, I'll level this reservation to nothing but rubble and snow. You got it?"

"Just come and get your diamonds."

Shepard didn't say another word. He hung up, and the line went dead. Widow switched the phone off and stared at it. He wondered if it had a tracking chip in it, too. Regardless, he figured it was probably traceable. So he took the phone and slammed it into the wall, crushing it into tiny pieces.

"Why'd you do that?" Amita asked.

"In case he has a tracer in it."

"What if we need to talk to him again?"

"We won't. Either he'll be dead, or we will."

Jacobs said, "He won't let us go free."

Widow said, "We won't let him go free, either."

Amita said, "We need the state cops. I can't arrest them by myself."

Widow said, "No one's getting arrested."

43

THE TREES around the house were calm and top-heavy with snow. Wind blew and whistled through the branches of the tall trees. The air was filled with nature's icy breath. Off in the distance, Widow saw a deer stick its head up over a snowbank. The animal's antlers were enormous and ridged, its thick mane like a winter beard. Its eyes peered back at him, and then it cocked its head and looked off to the horizon. It suddenly stood tall and turned, darting away quickly into the gloom.

Widow watched it vanish, and turned his head to see what had frightened the deer away. He heard a low rumble in the sky. After about a minute, he saw a helicopter coming in low over the trees. It was a military stealth helicopter, the same one Jacobs had told him about. He wondered if it really was used in the raid on Bin Laden. Whatever. It didn't really matter at the moment, because his biggest concern was the machine gun attached to it. He watched as the helicopter yawed and stopped, hovering a moment, and then turned and circled.

The helicopter moved toward the rear of the house, near where he was hiding. It was a big black thing, a huge mechanical bird circling above its prey. Even in the gloom and snowy air, he could see the black polish glimmer.

Widow waited.

He had the G36 strapped over his shoulder. He stared up around the corner of the house at the stealth helicopter, waiting for the perfect moment. As soon as he was sure that the pilot could see him, he would make his move.

44

SHEPARD PEERED out the window of the cockpit of the Comanche RAH-70. He studied the two-story house. The pilot circled it. There was no clear place to land. The trees were too high and thick. There was a nice-sized front yard, but long branches from the nearest trees blocked it. The pilot turned to Shepard and said, "Nowhere to land, sir."

Shepard stayed quiet.

The guys in the back of the helicopter stared forward. Their night-vision goggles were turned up, not on because of the coming daylight, and their gear was on. They were ready to deploy.

Shepard said, "Prepare to fire the gun. We'll kill them in the house and take the whole thing down."

One of his guys said, "What about the diamonds? And Jacobs?"

Shepard said, "That little bastard will be dead with the rest of them. We'll hike back up and sift through the rubble ourselves for the diamonds."

The other guy leaned forward in his seat. The harness on his seat belt moved forward with him in a smooth arc. He asked, "What about the Indians?"

Shepard looked over to the pilot and asked, "How many rounds we got left for the Vulcan gun?"

The pilot smirked and said, "Plenty."

Shepard said, "After we kill Jacobs, we'll go back to the town and kill them while they sleep." Shepard smiled at the thought of massacring Native Americans. *Wouldn't be the first time*, he said to himself.

The pilot circled one last time and then yawed and prepared to fire the machine gun at the house.

45

"Stop!" Shepard shouted and pointed at a figure near the side of the house.

The pilot removed his finger from the trigger and looped the helicopter around to get a closer look. They saw Widow and two others on horseback. They darted off into the trees. The horses moved more slowly in the snow than they would have on flat ground, but still plenty fast.

"Follow them!" Shepard ordered.

The pilot didn't flinch. He effortlessly moved the helicopter up a little higher and throttled it in the direction Widow had been headed.

Shepard peered out the window and caught glimpses of what looked like three people and two horses running away through the trees. They were dark shadows, moving fast, but he could still make them out in the darkness.

The helicopter sustained a steady speed. They flew after Widow for a good ten minutes. The air around the rotors was slightly gusty, but conditions were close to optimal for a chase. No way could Widow outrun them on a horse. Maybe in the summer, on flat ground with trees to cover their escape, this plan would've worked, but no way was it going to save them from Shepard now.

The air outside the helicopter was relatively calm, but icy. The steel exterior of the aircraft was cold to the touch, but inside, Shepard and his crew were warm. They swiveled and turned and flew forward, catching glimpses of Widow and the other two through the trees. They tracked after the group for ten minutes, climbing higher and higher as the terrain turned mountainous. Then the helicopter slowed, and Shepard peered down again.

The pilot asked, "Where did they go?"

Shepard searched and then saw them dart off again from the trees in a different direction. The figures moved to the north.

"There!" Shepard said and pointed.

The pilot pivoted in his seat and swung the helicopter around. They flew off after them for another thirty seconds, then stopped and stared—faces blank.

The trees had opened up to a clearing. The occupants of the helicopter watched through the windows as Widow stopped the horses. He dismounted his horse and swatted at its rear.

He was completely alone. The other horse had no riders. Widow had led them away from the house.

AMITA AND MIKE JACOBS waited in the bathroom on the second floor of the house. They had done exactly as Widow asked. He had told them to go upstairs and lie in the bathtub. If Shepard fired the helicopter's gun on the house as he had at the previous house where Jacobs had hidden out, then the bathtub would be the safest place. The house had a huge cast iron tub, probably dating back to the eighteenth century. Very solid and durable. If anything in the house could provide cover from M50 ammunition, it would be that tub. Widow had his doubts that even iron would be enough, but he planned to draw the helicopter away and not give it a chance to shoot at the house.

THE SCAR across Shepard's face was pure white in contrast to his crimson in his cheeks. He was enraged at the fact that Widow had duped him with the oldest trick in the book. He had led them away from Jacobs and the woman cop with a trick that outdated the dinosaurs. Shepard's guys looked at each other but made no comments about the situation. They knew better. One word out of their mouths, and he'd throw them out of the helicopter, no questions asked. The ground was at least a hundred feet below them. The fall would kill them or break their backs at a minimum.

Shepard yelled, "Kill that bastard!"

The pilot smiled and jerked back the trigger of the machine gun. His method went against his training—years of military service had taught him always to squeeze, not pull the trigger—but he felt that this was a situation that called for pulling it. The Vulcan machine gun rotated and spun, spraying bullets. The mechanical noise of a whipping helicopter's rotors accompanied by the deafening sound of the gunshots bursting forth from the barrels echoed across the treetops. And the canon's muzzle flashed bright and orange. Bullets sprayed in a wide cone from the gun and tore through the trees. Wood splintered and cracked. Branches swayed and fractured as the bullets ripped through. Snow-banks exploded into powder as the rounds buried themselves deep in the ground.

Shepard smiled, knowing that Widow had to be dead.

48

WIDOW HAD no intention of dying in the northern territory of Wyoming, and certainly not at the hands of a madman like Alex Shepard.

Widow pulled in and hugged close to a massive tree trunk. The bark was solid black and felt devoid of life. He heard the mechanical cracking sound of the chain gun as bullets let loose from the helicopter. They fired out and rocketed past him. All around him, tree bark exploded, and snow burst into the air, fogging up any visibility that once existed.

Widow was relieved that the horses had run in the opposite direction. At least those poor animals would be safe from Shepard and his insanity.

The bullets, the crackling machine, and the orange fire that haloed around the muzzle seemed to go on forever. Widow's head rattled from the sound, and his bones vibrated. The bullets continued to assault the surrounding trees, piercing through everything within range. The gunfire went on and on until finally the machine gun ran out of bullets. Widow could hear the gun rattling as the empty cylinders rotated and then stopped.

That was when he smiled. He knew guns, and he knew the Vulcan machine gun mounted on the helicopter took about fifteen minutes to reload. And fifteen minutes in a firefight was a long time. The battle had changed hands. The advantage had shifted. Wars were fought and won in less than fifteen minutes.

Widow peered out from behind the tree, trying to locate the helicopter's position. He spotted it easily less than twenty yards away from him and maybe fifty feet above the ground. He had two options—to stay or to run. If he crept away and then took off running, he might just make it.

But all hope was dashed when he saw Shepard's next move.

The helicopter hovered, and the side door slid open. A long, black rope dropped out and hit the ground. One of Shepard's guys leaped out of the opened door onto the rope and fast-roped toward the ground. A second guy showed himself, covering his friend's descent with his Heckler and Koch G36. The silenced barrel moved from side to side. There was no chance of Widow getting a shot at the descending guy. Not with his buddy covering him. Even if he could hit the guy, there was no guarantee of taking him out. Both guys appeared to be wearing heavy SWAT gear and probably had some serious Kevlar on underneath.

Widow would have to step out from behind the tree—fast—and fire. If he hit the guy in the head, that would kill him. The distance wasn't a problem for such a fast shot. But the disturbed snow still filled the air and made the shot difficult because his target wasn't completely in focus. Not to mention the fact they wouldn't be motionless targets as they fast-roped down a rope.

Before Widow could plan a second approach, the first guy was on the ground. He dropped to the ground on his knee and pointed his gun out, sweeping the area. The second guy leaped out of the open door and fast-roped down. He was fast. Shepard came out last.

Now Widow had three CIA-trained opponents with superior firepower, air support, and night-vision goggles. He ducked back behind the tree and looked down at the G36. He suddenly felt outgunned.

49

SHEPARD TOOK THE LEAD, moving forward in an awkward, hunched fashion.

Shepard was from a different generation of soldiers. He had been taught to approach a hostile environment by shooting first. His guys had been trained to stay safe first, to keep their guns low, to avoid friendly fire. It was a concept Shepard didn't understand.

The three men walked into the forest for about twenty yards. Behind Shepard and to his right, one guy crept along, covering the right flank. The helicopter had recoiled and rose higher into the sky. The pilot hovered and circled the area to give them a bird's-eye view. Shepard was the only one with an earpiece and radio that gave him direct communication with the pilot.

One of the other men held grenades.

The guy on the right had the backup magazines. He was to carry extra supplies, which made him feel like the least important member of the squad, but it was better than being dead. He had his G36, his Glock, and a Ka-Bar 1280 Combat Kukri Blade with a black Kraton G handle. The blade was eight and a half inches long and sharp. It was an unusual knife because of its long blade that curved inward. It was his lucky knife, and he had served with it for years.

He looked back at Shepard and saw he was giving the signal for them to split up—Shepard would go straight, and the two men would cover the left and right quadrants. The rule had always been to go thirty-five yards and no farther, but in this case, he knew the rule had changed to "don't come back until Widow is dead."

He moved to the right. The wind howled and echoed through the trees and fresh bullet holes. It gusted and blew across his face. He walked on for thirty yards. Then thirty-five. Then he felt a voice in the back of his head saying, *Too far. Too far.* He stopped and peered back over his shoulder. He could still see his partner's back. So he about-faced and moved forward.

The gloom was getting thicker in the forest, so he reached up and pulled down his goggles, clicking on the night vision. The device hummed, and his field of vision turned bright green. He could see much better and would notice if anything moved.

He continued on.

The gloom increased. It engulfed him. He turned to look over his shoulder, searching for his partners again—no sign of them. Their snow-colored gear had backfired on them in this environment because they were camouflaged too well and couldn't see each other. And now they were limited in the directions they could fire. If he fired his weapon in a southern cone, he might hit his friend—or worse, Shepard. That would be bad for him. Very bad.

He turned forward again and pressed on.

50

WIDOW WATCHED THE GUY. He remained in the shadows and followed him with his eyes. Widow had found a man-sized hole at the base of a tree. It felt like a shallow grave. He had jumped in and pulled snow down toward him as best he could. He felt he was packed in well enough to hide his bulk.

He watched as the clumsy mercenary approached. The guy seemed terrified. He wanted to open fire and kill him where he stood, but he couldn't. He had a silencer. But a silencer on an assault rifle, like a G36C, isn't silent at all. The sound from it probably would've echoed between the trees, and the others would've heard it. Plus, the muzzle flash would've been like a bright bolt of lightning cracking through the sky. It would give away his position.

Widow could smell the cold, watery scent of snow mingled with the remaining smoke from the Vulcan's gunfire. It still hung in the air—pungent and acrid. He watched the guy move in closer to him. He was too far away for Widow to grab him, which had been his plan. Grab the guy fast, drop him to his knees, and silence him. But something even better presented itself. The guy had passed Widow without even a second look, so he dragged himself out of the hole and crept up behind him. The soft snow quieted his steps.

Ten feet from him, Widow saw the knife sheathed at the small of the guy's back. In five fluid moves and a single agonizing one, the guy was dead. *One*. Widow stepped forward. *Two*. He clasped his enormous hand over the guy's mouth. *Three*. He unsheathed the Ka-Bar. *Four*. He sliced it across the guy's neck, severing his vestibular and vocal folds. *Five*. He jerked the blade straight out and let him drop to the ground. And *six*. The guy gurgled and rolled on the ground as he exsanguinated.

Widow could've helped him. He could've killed him quickly, but in the end, he thought about the dead dog from earlier. And Widow liked dogs. Instead of helping the guy, he watched him die.

After the guy was dead, Widow spat on the corpse.

* * *

THE OTHER MAN had walked the farthest away from Shepard. He wasn't scared of Widow. But he feared Shepard.

He swept his area thoroughly and found no sign of anyone. No footprints. No noise.

His quadrant seemed to have suffered the most damage from the helicopter's gunfire. If Widow had been hiding here, he was dead. And if he had survived the firefight, he would've been hit by a few bullets for sure—no doubt about that. But if that was the case, his blood would've been on the snow. But he saw nothing. He figured Widow was dead somewhere or had headed in one of the other directions.

He was just about to give up when he heard a whisper. He turned. His goggles showed a vast green figure hulking in front of him. He thought it was a bear, but he saw no claws, just one big, long one. And before he could react, Widow stabbed the Ka-Bar straight into his neck, just above where the collarbone dipped down. With his other hand, he swiped the guy's G36. The second guy went down like a marionette whose strings had been cut. His hand clawed and scratched at his throat as he tried to pull the knife out.

Widow raised one heavy foot over him and stomped down on the Ka-Bar's hilt, burying the blade straight into the back of the guy's neck like a hammer hitting a nail. The guy stopped moving, and Widow spat on him as well. *After all*, he thought to himself, *I'm not sure who killed the dog—no reason to discriminate now.*

He knelt down and pulled the knife out of the guy's neck and wiped the blood off on the guy's white jacket. Then he searched him. He found a pouch with three grenades. They were fragmentation grenades. Each was the size of a snow-ball. He smiled.

51

A FRAGMENTATION GRENADE is packed with deadly projectiles that explode outward after the pin has been pulled and the device is thrown. It's an old and elementary military weapon. The fragmentation grenade is the very definition of the phrase "If it ain't broke, don't fix it?"

Widow took the silencer out of his pocket and tossed it. It was useless to him now. There were three grenades on the dead guy, but he figured why bog himself down with extra weight. So he took one and shoved it in his pocket.

He scanned the cloudy area and saw nothing but trees and smoke. There was no sign of Shepard. Widow crept along the footpath made by the last dead guy, following it back to its origin, where the three mercenaries had fast-roped from the helicopter. Once there, he paused and examined the area. Still no sign of movement, but he saw Shepard's footprints in the snow. That was the good thing about tracking someone in the snow—footprints are obvious. However, Widow was far from a fool. He wasn't about to get double bluffed by his own tactic from earlier. And Alex Shepard was a professional veteran of the CIA. He was no idiot. Since Widow didn't trust any kind of obvious trail left for him by Shepard, he took a fresh approach. Instead of engaging Shepard in the dark, he headed toward the sound of the helicopter's rotors.

The closer he got to the helicopter's position, the more the smoke and snow lifted from the ground because of the prop wash from the rotors' ferocious spin. He took the long way around, staying clear of the helicopter's spotlight and out of the pilot's view. Slowly and steadily, he walked, keeping behind trees and snowbanks.

Widow looked up at the helicopter. It was a frightening thing. Black with a shimmer that looked almost like black chrome. The machine had certainly been used to terrify villagers in Syria and other parts of the Middle East. But this wasn't the Middle East, and Widow was no villager.

Widow scrambled one last time through the smoke and leaned his back against a nearby tree. He was directly beneath the helicopter. He could see that it didn't have a tail number—no way for it to be tracked or identified.

Widow measured the distance between the helicopter and the ground in his mind. It was too high. He needed to get the pilot to lower it. That meant losing the element of surprise, which wasn't a good idea when dealing with a military attack helicopter. He reevaluated his plan.

At least two things were on his side. First, the helicopter's side door was still open, and second, the tree directly behind it had low branches. Instead of trying to get the helicopter lower, he would go higher.

Widow ducked down and waited until the pilot rotated the helicopter to face the other direction, which he was doing every thirty seconds. As soon as the cockpit faced the opposite direction, Widow darted to the tree with the low branches and leaped as high as he could, which wasn't far because of the snow. He barely reached the lowest limb. He pulled up and heaved himself onto the branch.

Widow climbed. Fast. He reached a spot midway up the tree and saw that the helicopter was within throwing distance. He steadied himself, remembered his grenade training.

He held his breath, pulled the grenade out of his pocket, and yanked the pin, releasing it to fall and clatter against the tree and tumble to the ground. He aimed and threw the grenade, which spun as it flew toward the helicopter. It flew forty feet, forty-five, then forty-seven. The helicopter continued rotating, and the grenade bounced, barely, in through the open door. The pilot heard the noise and looked out the window. His eyes connected with Widow's, and then he craned his head around and saw what had made the bouncing noise behind him in the cabin. He never turned his head back around to face forward. He never got the chance because the grenade exploded.

At the same time that the grenade exploded, Widow knew the explosion would give away his position, bring the bad guys to him. So he didn't wait to see what happened. He clambered down the tree as quick as he could. He knew Shepard would be coming. Widow grabbed branch after branch, descending downward, jostling and scrambling his way back down the tree like a spider rushing backward.

The helicopter exploded and fell as Widow clambered down the tree.

Violently, the helicopter's windshield erupted in a fury of broken glass and blood. Then the helicopter's metal skeleton expanded and ripped. And the front door blew off. It flung out into the trees. The rotors exploded and twisted like two broke arms. They swivelled erratically before stopping dead in the air. The helicopter twisted and spun and plunged to the ground below. It dropped and tumbled sixty-five feet to the forest floor. The bird didn't explode when it crashed, not like in the movies. It just fell like deadweight. The force of the crash crushed the helicopter's roof inward upon impact. One blade broke and snapped at the midpoint. It tumbled off into the forest. The starboard side collapsed and imploded, and black smoke mushroomed out. The crashing sound boomed and echoed between the trees and the snow. It sounded like a monstrous tree toppling over.

Widow reached the bottom of the tree and stopped. He scanned all the points on the compass, looking for any signs of the enemy in case they were early. There was none. He scanned again, this time for a hiding place, until he found one. He scrambled to over to it. It was the perfect place for an ambush. It was somewhere Shepard wouldn't suspect him to be. He huddled to it and waited.

Widow smiled to himself and thought, *One left.*

52

SHEPARD WAS a twenty-year veteran with a spy agency. He was well trained and dangerous. He never thought he would meet someone who could single-handedly take out his crew and a military attack helicopter.

He ran toward the sound as fast as he could and made it to the wreckage within minutes. Perhaps he should've approached more cautiously, but Shepard wasn't thinking about his training, only his anger. He stopped with his jaw open and stared at the crumpled steel and bent tail of the helicopter. The blood and the wreckage stared back at him. He stared at the twisted metal and the shattered glass that was sprayed out over the snow. He couldn't understand how Widow had done this.

Shepard stood there and glared at the wreckage in disbelief. His guys were all dead, leaving him all alone. He grabbed his G36 and started firing blindly into the surrounding trees. The silencer whizzed and purred as bullets sprayed out. He fired in a rage. The bullets slammed into the trees surrounding Widow's hiding place. Some ricocheted in the smoky darkness, drilling themselves into far-off trees.

Shepard squeezed the trigger until the gun clicked empty. Then he ejected the magazine and reloaded. But before he could reload, Widow revealed himself.

At first, Shepard was relieved when he saw a hulking figure climb out of the helicopter wreckage. He thought his pilot had survived, but then he realized that the bulky silhouette wasn't his pilot. It was Widow.

Widow stood in the wreckage of the helicopter like one of those terminators from the movies who walk away from disaster completely unscathed. He pointed a G36 straight at Shepard. He said in a calm but cold voice, "You're done here."

Shepard tossed his weapon and lifted his hands in surrender.

Widow said, "Now the sidearm and the vest."

Shepard moved slowly. He unsnapped his Kevlar vest and let it slip off. It bounced slightly on the snow. Then he removed his sidearm and ejected the magazine and tossed the gun farther off into the darkness. He grinned and asked, "Who the hell are you?"

"Me? You saw my file. Maybe you should've looked closer. Or maybe you didn't see all of it. Maybe you don't have as much clout at the agency like you think. The guy in that file is who I used to be. Now I'm nobody. Just a guy. But not a guy you should've messed with."

Silence fell between them.

Shepard asked, "What now? You going to call the cops? You got plenty of evidence."

Widow shook his head and said, "No cops. You'd just get out of that somehow. Evidence or not. No, I got a better idea."

Shepard looked blank.

"I'll give you a fighting chance," Widow said.

He lowered the gun and tossed it into the wreckage behind him. Then he brandished the P99 and ejected the magazine. He frowned at the fact that he had never gotten to use it, but this was the better way. He tossed the gun blindly into the dark.

Shepard smiled because Widow had just made a huge mistake. He was an expert in hand-to-hand combat. Widow was going down. Shepard grinned and charged Widow.

But Widow had never promised a fair fight. He was a former SEAL and had been trained to win. So he cheated without hesitation. As soon as Shepard was within reaching distance, Widow pulled the Ka-Bar out from behind the waistband of his pants, cocked his left arm all the way back, and with all of his strength, plunged it forward as he side-stepped to the right. The blade sliced through Shepard's face and lodged in his skull in the opposite direction of his scar.

X marks the spot, Widow thought. It would've left a very interesting scar if he had lived, but he didn't because Widow had hit him harder than the guy who gave him the first scar had. And the Ka-Bar was very sharp. The blade cracked through Shepard's skull and punctured his brain. Shepard fell to the snow and twisted and jerked. Widow watched him until he was dead.

He didn't spit on Shepard's body. No need. He was done here.

53

WIDOW STAYED in Tower Junction the next night. He rented a motel room and slept most of the morning away. He woke up to a message from the desk clerk. *Terry's Diner*, it read.

Widow got dressed in the same clothes and left his room with no intention of ever seeing it again. He walked from the motel and turned one corner and then another until he reached Main Street, then he continued on until he came to 113 Main Street. Terry's Diner.

Amita's police cruiser was in the parking lot. He entered the diner and saw the waitress from the other day. He looked around the room and saw Amita sitting in the corner booth with Mike Jacobs. They held hands like old lovers, which disappointed Widow. He felt a little heartache, a little disheartened by it. But that's life.

Widow walked over to them and said hello, then sat with his back to the door for the second time, ignoring his normal practice with Amita, but he saw no harm in it at the moment. After all, life was about embracing change.

Amita said, "Hi."

"Hello," Widow said. "I see you two are doing well."

Jacobs smiled and said, "Thanks to you."

Amita smiled at Widow as well and asked, "Are you hungry? Order something. It's on us."

"I'm good," Widow lied. He didn't want to impose.

Amita said, "We haven't decided what to do about this situation. What do you think?"

"Do nothing. They'll show up on their own."

Jacobs said, "The CIA's already shown up. They came in as soon as the storm settled."

Amita said, "You were asleep."

"What did you tell them?"

"Nothing. They came in with FBI badges. My father gave them the runaround. He's still doing it. So far, he's just denying knowing anything."

Widow nodded.

Jacobs said, "He is taking credit for defending his reservation against a horde of unknown, armed forces."

Amita asked, "What would you have done?"

"I would have said nothing. I would've told them I never heard of Alex Shepard—or Mike Jacobs. Or better yet, I would've moved the bodies out there around the helicopter and tossed a grenade in it. Then I would've called the state police and told them the townspeople heard a helicopter crash in the woods during the snowstorm."

Amita asked, "Would they've bought that?"

Widow smiled. "The CIA will buy anything and cover it up, anyway. They always do. They aren't going to want any attention on Shepard and his enterprise."

Widow looked at Jacobs and continued. "But you have to leave. Go somewhere else. Change your name. They won't look for you. Hell, they'd probably even help you remain hidden just to bury the truth."

Amita looked at Jacobs and said, "I don't want to lose him again."

"Give it a month or two, then join him. You wanted to leave the reservation, anyway. Those were your words."

Silence came over them, and Amita and Jacobs smiled at each other like the decision had already been made for them. Now they'd be able to plan the life they had always wanted together.

Widow broke the silence.

"What happened to the boy?"

"The CIA wanted to take him."

"Did they?"

Jacobs said, "No. I called the Mexican consulate in Denver. Then I called ICE and the US Marshals. I wasn't sure about the jurisdiction here. I was also afraid of the CIA's reach. So I decided it was safer for him to be checked out by everyone I could think of instead of just calling one federal agency and leaving it up to chance that someone on the CIA's payroll might be in the chain of command. I tried to put as many eyes on the boy's safety as I could. As of right now, the Mexican government is working with the State Department to get him back to his family."

"He gonna be ok?"

"I think so. Sure. In the long run. I'm ashamed of my part in it all."

"Don't be. You're the reason that little boy is alive at all."

Jacobs said nothing to that.

Widow thought to ask about the diamonds, but he had a hunch that they would be reported lost to the CIA or denied altogether. He had a hunch the diamonds would make a nice starter life for Amita and Jacobs. And he figured they would think of that too. So he didn't ask.

They sat in silence for a moment while Widow drank coffee till the cup was bone dry.

Amita looked at Widow. "Where will you go?"

Widow stared into the empty void of his cup, and for a moment, Amita thought he might lick it clean, like a lizard. But he didn't.

He said, "Wherever the road takes me."

Widow shoved his hands into his pockets and pulled out a crumpled wad of cash-money, uncrumpled it, and flattened it under the empty coffee mug. He left the cash there on the table to cover the bill and the tip.

Widow stood up tall and said no goodbye. He gave them no last look, no goodbye nods. He just turned and walked out of the diner, leaving Amita and Jacobs to themselves, to their own paths, to their own lives.

Out on the street, Widow shivered from an icy breeze that swept across his face. He walked over to the next street and stopped at a crosswalk. He looked up and down the street, both directions, east and west. To the east, there was a highway cloverleaf, the perfect place to catch a ride. He glanced west and saw a group of buses huddled together. A Greyhound bus station. Another good choice.

A WORD FROM SCOTT

Thank you for reading *Winter Territory*. You got this far—I'm guessing that you enjoyed Widow.

The story continues in a fast-paced series that takes Widow (and you) all around the world, solving crimes, righting wrongs.

The next book, *A Reason to Kill*, has Widow drifting along a sweltering Texas landscape. Everything is good until he gets charged with locating a missing child. His investigation leads to a deadly political conspiracy. Widow races against the clock to save the child from dangerous murderers who will kill to keep the truth in the dark.

The fourth book (one of my personal favorites) is *Without Measure*. Hitchhiking all night. No sleep. Widow stops in a diner in a California mountain town. A chance meeting with a Marine officer. A short conversation. And an hour later, the Marine walked onto a military base, shot and killed five random people, and committed suicide. Now, the

MPs want to know why. All suspicion is on the outsider, Widow. In this exciting mystery, Widow digs deep under the surface to uncover the truth. As he turns over rocks, he finds dark secrets crawling underneath.

What are you waiting for? The fun is just starting. Once you start Widow, you won't be able to stop.

A REASON TO KILL:
A PREVIEW

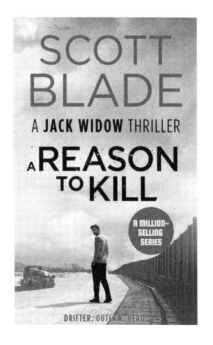

Out now!

A REASON TO KILL:
A BLURB

A missing young girl.

A horrifying conspiracy.

Jack Widow will kill to save her.

Widow hunts across Texas for an abducted child in the riveting third novel in Scott Blade's Amazon bestselling Jack Widow series.

Drifting along a sweltering Texas landscape, Widow waits at a dusty bus station, when he meets Claire Hood, a grandmother, clearly in distress. Claire is on a solo mission to rescue her abducted granddaughter.

If that wasn't enough, the next thing that happens is unthinkable. Claire drops dead—natural causes. Right there in front of Widow.

Widow isn't the kind of guy to let wrongs go. He picks up her bus ticket and takes her place on a quest that will give him a reason to kill.

Readers are saying...

★★★★★ A binge-worthy series!

★★★★★ Jack Widow is awesome!

CHAPTER 1

Jack Widow had no reason to kill anybody.

Not now. Not recently. Not yet. Killing had been the last thing on his mind. He was traveling. Seeing. Experiencing. Touristing. Taking things in.

Making memories.

One memory, the one that wouldn't leave him, was two days ago. Back in a hotel room, Widow had been tangled in bleached sheets with high thread counts and soft limbs, and bare and naked with a beautiful woman in Las Vegas.

The impression lasted. He had a smile on his face for the entire two days that followed.

The feeling he held on to was the opposite of retribution. The reverse of reprisal. The contradiction of payback. The disagreement of disagreement.

It was sunshine in the dark.

He was the farthest thing from wanting to kill.

In the sweltering Texas heat, that was all about to change.

He first met Claire Hood outdoors in a bus depot in West Texas.

She was a nice old bird, as nice as old birds come, like the catalog version of a sweet grandmother, and nothing else. She didn't have a mean bone in her body—not a mean word from her lips.

She was like a churchly grandmother who baked cookies for everyone on her block and then returned after a couple of days to recover the plastic ware and ask if everyone had enjoyed the cookies. She left no stomachs and no lives untouched.

She was the kind of woman who played bingo every Tuesday and Thursday night, routine. At least that's what she told her family. In reality, she was gambling. Playing pinochle, sometimes bridge, sometimes poker with her friends.

She belonged in a Kodak photo of a family picnic more than she did sitting on a hot, dry bus terminal bench close to the wasteland part of Texas on the long stretch of Interstate 10, somewhere between El Paso and San Antonio.

But that's where she was. Right there. She sat on a bus station bench, filled with nothing but bravery and pride. The sensation beamed off her. She seemed a little haughty, a little superior to the rest of the ticket holders. Not too far. Not in an arrogant I'm-better-than-thou kind of way, but borderline.

She sat upright on the edge of her seat, back straight and chin up. Perfect posture. Her purse rested on her knees like a small dog. A perfectly pint-sized black hat rested on her head. Her gaunt hands were stacked, palm on top of palm, across her lap.

Her shoes were leathery and almost crinkle free, old but not worn to the point of retirement.

Her eyes were brown, and she had tan, paperlike skin. Lighter than her shoes, but not by much. She was a skinny thing: skin and bones, only more bones than skin. Her gray hair curled and coiled and merged with whiter strands of hair, all of which punched out from under the brim of her hat.

All the things Widow noticed about her had been his first and last impressions of her. Because twenty-one minutes after they met, after a long, revealing conversation, Claire Hood dropped dead.

A SPECIAL OFFER

Get your copy of Night Swim: a Jack Widow Novella.
Available only at ScottBlade.com

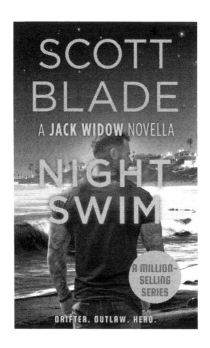

NIGHT SWIM: A BLURB

Under the cover of night, Widow swims through dangerous waters to rescue an FBI agent from a death sentence.

A blown cover for an FBI agent means a death sentence, unless Widow can stop it.

Under cover of darkness along the Malibu coast, Widow takes a night swim. It's meant to be soothing and stress-relieving.

Instead, Widow's night swim turns deadly with the echo of gunshots over open water. A covert FBI operation is blown apart, leaving only blood in the water and a lone undercover agent exposed to a den of lethal international criminals. From the quiet night swim to a high-stakes criminal party at a mega millionaire's beach house, Widow faces grave danger to warn her.

Widow, the drifter who stands for justice, emerges from the waves. With literally nothing but his resolve, he faces unbelievable odds. Time is running out, the enemy is within reach, and for Widow, stealth and cunning are his only weapons.

In this pulse-pounding Widow novella, the line between the hunter and the hunted blurs in a deadly game of espionage and survival.

THE SCOTT BLADE BOOK CLUB

Fostering a connection with my readers is the highlight of my writing journey. Rest assured, I'm not one to crowd your inbox. You'll only hear from me when there's exciting news to share—like a fresh release hitting the shelves or a can't-miss promotion.

If you're just stepping into the world of Jack Widow, consider this your official invite to the Scott Blade Book Club. As a welcome gift, you'll receive the Night Swim: A Widow Novella in the starter kit.

By joining, you'll gain access to a trove of exclusive content, including free stories, special deals, bonus material, and the latest updates on upcoming Widow thrillers.

Ready to dive in? Visit ScottBlade.com to sign up and begin your immersion into the Widow universe.

THE NOMADVELIST

NOMAD + NOVELIST = NOMADVELIST

Scott Blade is a Nomadvelist, a drifter and author of the breakout Jack Widow series. Scott travels the world, hitch-hiking, drinking coffee, and writing.

Jack Widow has sold over a million copies.

Visit @: ScottBlade.com

Contact @: scott@scottblade.com

Follow @:

Facebook.com/ScottBladeAuthor

Bookbub.com/profile/scott-blade

Amazon.com/Scott-Blade/e/B00AU7ZRS8

ALSO BY SCOTT BLADE

The Jack Widow Series

Gone Forever

Winter Territory

A Reason to Kill

Without Measure

Once Quiet

Name Not Given

The Midnight Caller

Fire Watch

The Last Rainmaker

The Devil's Stop

Black Daylight

The Standoff

Foreign and Domestic

Patriot Lies

The Double Man

Nothing Left

The Protector

Kill Promise

The Shadow Club

The Ghost Line

Jack Widow Shorts

Night Swim

Printed in Great Britain
by Amazon

a589f8d4-7af8-4405-af6e-81b6a36d0b2aR01